THE MISSING LINK

The Missing Link

Copyright 2024 By J K Brogdon

First Edition - October 2024

This is a work of fiction. Names, characters, places, and incidents are either the product of the author's imagination or used fictitiously. Any resemblance to actual persons living or dead, or actual events is purely coincidence.

Cover Design: Nimra Bukhari
Published by "Independently Published"

ACKNOWLEDGEMENTS

This book would not have been possible without the support and encouragement of several amazing people!

First, I want to thank my husband for putting up with me every night and on weekends working on this book. He knew the importance of this book and never complained and always encouraged me!

I also want to thank my daughter, Emily, who was the first to read and edit my book and give me insightful suggestions and asked questions where the manuscript didn't make sense. Thank you for all the support! Thank you to my daughter, Katie, for the support through social media and always encouraging me to not stop.

Thank you to my other editing team: Jim and Barbara Barnes and Nell for reading, discussing, making marginal notes and helping with grammar and giving other perspectives of the characters. Your expertise helped shape this book into what it is today.

To all my friends and family for all the encouragement and support.

Finally, to every reader who takes a chance on "The Missing Link"-thank you for joining me on this journey. I hope you find as much joy in reading it as I did in writing it.

This book is dedicated to those who love me.

I appreciate those who cheered me on and encouraged and had patience with me. I also appreciate those who may have helped me develop characters without even knowing it!

It's also dedicated to my cat, Sammy!

CHAPTER 1

Reggie couldn't shake the confusion as news spread of a Chicago reporter traveling to Georgia. After all, she was uncertain whether any crime had even happened. A local girl was reported missing, but Reggie found herself questioning the situation - was she truly in danger, or had she simply chosen to stay away from home?

Reggie leaned up against her jeep, lighting her last cigarette from a pack she bought yesterday at the Handy Mart. She stuck her finger in the pack just to make sure it was empty. "Damn, my last one already."

She pulled her long strawberry blonde hair up in a ponytail, fanning herself with her cowboy hat from the heat of the day. Beads of sweat glistened on her forehead. She was thankful July 4th had come and gone. It was the busiest one yet. Several of the locals had been arrested for fighting and public intoxication, causing a riot. They were on Main street revving the engines of their loud trucks having their own "4th of July parade," when they turned on each other. Reggie wasn't sure who threw the first punch but it ended up with trucks and egos damaged. July 4th or any holiday had never been something she looked forward to while growing up. Most of her holidays were spent with her parents being drunk and fighting or were nowhere around. Some holidays, she didn't know where they were but her grandparents would step in when they received a call from the sheriff.

It was Thanksgiving and she was 15, her parents were gone for at least three days with no communication until her father called her grandfather asking for a ride home from jail. She started living with her grandparents during that Thanksgiving holiday making her life so much easier. Her parents never did ask her to come home. She still worried about her parents but as time passed, she worried less and less. They didn't care about her so why should she care about them?

TJ parked his rental car, a compact Honda with no added on features. It was within the budget the news station had given him. He did a quick glance at himself in the mirror and looked at his watch, he was late. The rental car company at the airport was overwhelmed with customers which delayed his arrival. Why had he not arranged a car to pick him up at the airport, instead? He knew this was on company time and he needed to use their budget and follow their rules. He wasn't thrilled about coming to this small town but he knew something was happening and the story was here. As he walked closer to the old red brick building, which appeared to have been built in the 1950's, he saw a woman who looked almost posed leaning up against a jeep. She was tall, beautiful, wearing a t-shirt and jeans with a gun in a holster, holding a cowboy hat. He was definitely not in Chicago anymore.

Reggie looks up and sees a well-dressed, good looking man in a suit walking across the parking lot towards her. She takes a long draw, as she watches him, thinking to herself that neither he nor his suit are from around here, she inhales and blows the smoke straight up in the air as he approaches.

"Do you happen to know where I can find Detective Memphis?" he said looking at his watch.

Reggie threw her cigarette down the drain pipe as she walked up the sidewalk. "You're late but you found who you are looking for. Come to my office so we can talk."

He stopped and looked at her, "Oh, I thought,"

She quickly interrupted. "I know what you thought."

They walked in the side door down the dimly lit hallway with only a couple of offices on each side of the hall. Original wood floors, wide crown molding and framed portraits of previous sheriffs hung on the walls. One door had a sign on it that read: 'Sheriff Johnson', the other door read: Detective Memphis.

Reggie opened her office door. "Have a seat," motioning towards the chairs in front of her desk.

How many times has she dealt with people assuming Detective Reggie Memphis was a male? Most of the men in this town wished she was a male detective. Apparently, men are better at this sort of thing, according to the conversation she overheard at the farmer's market when she was first appointed by the Sheriff. She kept her mouth shut keeping her thoughts to herself.

"Now, which news station do you work for?" He lifted his credential badge up closer to her, It read - Terrence J. Jenkins, WTSJ.

"I work for Channel 4 news out of Chicago. I'm on assignment here indefinitely or until you solve this mystery."

He gave a half smile showing his dimples. He smelled good, the masculine, woodsy distinguished kind of smell.

"Well, tell me what you know so far."

Reggie wanted to find out what was being said about this in Chicago. She watched him as he took his suit jacket off. It was an expensive suit evidenced by the lining inside the jacket. He was well-groomed, a city guy, a good looking black man with an athletic build. She grabbed her bag of gummy bears, when he started to speak.

She interrupted, "You like gummy bears?"

"As a matter of fact, I do,"

She grabbed a handful then handed the bag over to him. He pulled out his phone to look at his notes and started reading out loud.

"Here is what I know - Ms. Bailey called me in Chicago. She is the aunt of the missing girl, Kendra. Her niece, Kendra, has been missing for over a week. She was last seen at the Wagon Wheel. She is 21- years-old and works at a flooring company. Ms. Bailey said 4 other teens in town have been missing for over a month and no one seems to know what happened." He looked up from his cell phone and then grabbed a handful of gummy bears."

"So, you are here because she said 4 now 5 people are missing from Birch Creek?" Reggie asked.

He shook his head saying "yes."

She stared at him for a long 10 seconds, still fanning herself with her cowboy hat. Then said, "you need to meet Ms. Bailey."

His eyes opened wide as he raised his eyebrows, "Ok, I'm not sure what you are trying to tell me". He smiled, showing that dimple again.

"You have come a long way here, I'm sure it's very different from Chicago." Reggie laughed. She handed him her card and said, "Go explore Birch Creek. We can talk tomorrow. I will walk you out."

She walked him out the front entrance past some of the deputies, the receptionist and Ed, the forensic analyst who all looked up at him as they walked by. TJ nodded his head towards them acknowledging he had their attention. Reggie knew they probably thought he was an FBI agent, he looked the part.

As he walked down the sidewalk to the parking lot, she watched him. He stopped, took out his phone and stared at it. He must have been reading a text. She waited until he drove away in his rental car to walk out to her jeep. It's a twenty year old jeep that she inherited from her grandfather when he passed away a few years back. She has to step up into it. It comes in handy around this country with its big tires and four-wheel drive. She ignores the chipping paint and rust spots. Her grandfather loved this jeep and she loves it just as much as he did.

TJ looked at his text again when he got into the car. It read: *"You were right, she is with him."* He didn't respond. It just confirmed what he already knew. Coming to this little country town is probably the best thing for me right now but not only was I late to meet Detective Memphis, I had insulted her too. He wasn't sure why but she intimidated him. Something about her, he thought. He decided to do just what Detective Memphis had suggested. He drove around the town of Birch Creek. He saw several "mom and pop" type restaurants. Birch Creek had a nice public park with well-maintained walking trails, fountains and picnic areas. He drove through the downtown area which took about two minutes. Bookstore, coffee shop, pizza place, gift shops and a salon, your typical small downtown. He liked what he saw and how it made him feel nostalgic. He grew up in Chicago but in his earlier years, he lived in a suburb of Chicago that had more of a hometown vibe.

He used to ride his bicycle to school every morning unless it was raining or snowing. I'm sure in this town, kids could still ride their bikes to school without parents having to worry. Now, living in the city of Chicago, he was used to walking everywhere from his penthouse. It wasn't the same as walking in a small town--the traffic was loud, people weren't friendly and everyone rushed to their destination. Also, there is the fear or anticipation of getting robbed by someone. TJ remembers when his mother had been mugged while shopping alone downtown years ago. She never has gotten over the fear she felt that day. They grabbed her purse, knocking her to the ground. She wasn't hurt but it scared her so much that she doesn't do that anymore. She mostly shops online or has her assistant take care of any shopping. The Chef does all the grocery shopping, she no longer has a reason to go downtown unless it's for dinner or a fundraising event. As TJ drove around the town, he realized there isn't a hotel here in Birch Creek. He pulled into the park, googled "hotels near me" and quickly realized he would be staying about 30 miles away.

Reggie drove north of town to what's referred to as the "rock church." It was built about seventy years ago and built with all rock. It's one of those direction markers that everyone understands when you tell them to turn by the rock church. It's a beautiful rock building, well maintained with a small congregation that keeps it looking great. She turned by the church on the road that turns to dirt as you head up the mountain. The Bailey's live at the foot of the mountain in a picturesque setting with a creek in the back behind their house. Their house is a nice mountain cabin with a wraparound porch and a big fireplace made of mountain rock that covers almost the whole side of the cabin. There is beautiful Mountain Laurel blooming alongside the creek and of course the awesome River Birch trees line the creek as well. Birch Creek was named after the River Birch trees that grow all along the river and the creeks. One day, this property is going to sell for a lot of money, Reggie thought to herself as she drove up the driveway. Reggie knows Ms. Bailey well. She has a criminal history with the Birch Creek Sheriff's Department.

She could see someone sitting on the front porch as she drove up and parked by the walkway leading up to the porch. She jumped down out of the jeep, waved her hand to let whomever it was on the porch know it was her before stepping onto the sidewalk.

"Hey, it's Reggie, I need to talk to you."

She heard Ms. Doris Bailey telling her to "come on up."

As Reggie topped the steep stairs on the porch, she caught her breath and saw Doris sitting in a rocking chair.

"Well, Regina, do you have any news for us about Kendra?" Doris sat up straight in the chair with her eyebrows raised.

"Unfortunately, No, Ms. Bailey, is Frank home too?"

"Frank's inside watching TV, probably sleeping!"

Reggie could see the glare of the TV as she peered into the window. It looked like a John Wayne western was on, she remembered her grandpa always loved John Wayne movies and he was so proud of his autographed photo of John Wayne that hung in the entrance hallway. Frank was sleeping as Doris had suggested.

"Ms. Bailey, I need to ask you a few questions if you don't mind." She didn't wait for an answer. She kept talking assuming it was ok to continue. "It seems like you have some more information than what you told me last week about Kendra. You called the News station in Chicago, why?" She paused, waiting on Doris to answer.

Doris Bailey had gained some weight now and looked much healthier than several years back when she was strung out on meth most of her waking hours. She had blown up a shed, accidentally, of course; trying to cook her own batch. That's when her boys went to live with their daddy in Florida.

She did some time in the county jail and actually that is what saved her life. She has been sober now for at least ten years and married Frank Bailey, who is probably ten years older than she. He has been good for her which is what she needed. She used to blame Reggie for her boys going to live with their dad, because Reggie was the one who had to arrest her. Back then she didn't take any ownership of her addiction, but she wasn't exactly in her right frame of mind either. Her boys are grown with their own families and don't come around much as far as Reggie knew.

"Yes, I called the Chicago news. I wanted the National news to give this some attention. They can help us find Kendra if we get some reporters here asking questions and it gets talked about on the news."

Kendra had been living with Doris and Frank for the last couple of years. Doris took her in when her momma kicked her out of the house for getting caught with drugs in her car. Kendra never would admit to using but Doris knew! As far as Reggie knows, Kendra hasn't been using since she got caught.

"Doris, why did you tell that reporter that four teens have been missing for over a month? You know they were partying up on the mountain and finally went home safe and sound, well sort of, they were malnourished and needed rest but nonetheless, they are home."

Doris looked up with a smile which showed her new dentures that she got after all her teeth had rotted out. "Did it work? Is the news paying attention?"

Reggie laughed, "well, I'll be damned, yes it worked, you got their attention. Ok, so this reporter, Mr. Terrence J Jenkins, said that you told him she was last seen at the Wagon Wheel ? What the hell is the wagon wheel? You didn't tell me this last week."

"She was seen on the last night of the Wagon Train, not the wagon wheel." Doris laughed and said she guessed she should have explained our week long wagon train events to this Chicago reporter.

Reggie nodded in agreement knowing it is now making more sense to her.

"Ok, tell me who saw her and what did they say and to whom did they tell this too?"

"Freddie told his aunt Janie that he saw Kendra with some new guy that he didn't know and she was clearly intoxicated. They were watching the fireworks and sitting on a blanket with some other people that he didn't know either."

"Are you referring to Freddie Jones?"

"Yes" Doris sighed, "I know what you are thinking but he seemed to know what he was talking about according to his aunt."

"We found her car parked in the back field at the saddle club. Her car seemed to be undisturbed, since she parked it that night. They are checking it out thoroughly just to make sure."

Reggie handed her card to Doris and told her to call her if she hears anything else.

"Has Frank talked to anyone about her? He might have heard something at the VFW Hall?" Reggie posed it as a question to Doris.

"Frank hasn't left here in a week, so I don't think he has talked to anyone. He seems to think she is just hanging out with this new boyfriend."

"Why don't you think that too?"

Doris was shaking her head no - "She would have called me by now."

"You know I need to explain the situation to Mr. Jenkins, the reporter, so he knows the truth," Reggie smiled. "Thank you, Ms. Bailey, I will be in touch."

Reggie walked back down the steps to the sidewalk. She looked over admiring the garden that Frank had planted and maintained. She yelled back up at Doris, "Looks like you got some tomatoes that are ripe, better pick them." Reggie climbed up in her jeep and started driving back into town. She was thinking about Kendra being with some new boyfriend, who was he? How did she meet him? Who were the others they were with that night? Why had her best friend, Shay, not told her about this. She needed to find Freddie Jones and talk with him. Last she remembered, he worked at the chicken houses on the south end of town. She reached for her cigarettes, damn, she needs to buy some more.

She pulled into the Handy Mart just in time to run into Mr. Williams.

"Well, if it isn't Regina Ann Memphis, how you doin' darlin'?" Mr. Williams asked loudly. He is hard of hearing and won't think about getting hearing aids.

"I'm well, and you?" She shouted.

"My crops are looking good this year, but man, it's getting hot," he said. Reggie had known Mr. Williams as long as she could remember. He always has the best corn crop.

"Stay cool", she said as she walked in the store.

There was a new clerk working that morning.

"I haven't seen you here before, are you a new employee?"

"Yes, I'm Natalie. This is my first week, I just moved here from Tennessee."

"Nice to meet you, I'm Reggie, the local detective for the Birch Creek Sheriff's Department. I hope you like Birch Creek so far?"

"I do like it, but some of the customers refer to me as the 'colored girl.' Is it 1964, here?"

In some ways, Birch Creek is still in 1964, Reggie agreed. She felt her face turning red.

"I am so sorry, but they will be nice to you," Reggie said as she picked up her new bag of gummy bears and asked for some Marlboro lights.

"We will just have to teach them that is wrong and offensive. I will come back in a day or two and check on you, Welcome to Birch Creek." Reggie took her change and walked out of the door shaking her head in embarrassment of the customers but really not shocked at all.

Reggie lit her cigarette and drove towards the south end of the county. She called Shay, Kendra's best friend whom she had talked to last week already.

Shay spoke softly, "I'm at work and can't talk or I will get docked my pay for taking a break right now, I will have to call you back when my shift ends."

"Ok, sorry, sounds good." Reggie said as she hung up the phone. Shay worked at one of the local carpet mills and Reggie knew how strict they were about employees not taking calls during their shifts, it was for safety reasons.

While driving down the two lane highway she got behind one of the wagons being pulled by mules that had obviously been a part of the Wagon Train last week. The wagon pulled slightly off the road to let her pass, it was Emory Walls. She recognized him right away with his cowboy hat and big mustache that curled up on both sides. His mustache was stained a yellowish brown color from all the years of smoking. She pulled up and motioned to him to pull over at the Calvary Baptist Church parking lot so she could ask him a question. This two lane highway is a dangerous road with no shoulder on either side, car crashes happen all the time on this stretch of the road.

"Hey Emory, sorry to make you stop but I have a question - Do you remember seeing Kendra Bailey last week at Wagon Train?"

Emory's hands gripped the reins as he was trying to keep the mules steady. The strength of the mules was on full display as his knuckles were turning white.

"I saw her one night but I don't remember which night, I heard she was missing." Emory responded.

"Did you see her with anyone?"

"I don't remember, I didn't really pay attention. I saw a lot of people all week. I can ask around and see if anyone else remembers anything else about her."

"I would appreciate it." The mules jumped when a truck horn honked as it drove by. Emory was yelling at the mules to settle down.

"Ok, if you think of anything else that may come to mind about her, or hear anything else, let me know." Reggie said as she started walking back to her jeep.

"Will do," Emory shouted. Reggie waited a few minutes to let Emory get back on the road. She watched as the mules walked in unison at a steady pace. Emory's wagon was outfitted for camping, cooking and fun trail rides. He had all kinds of supplies, like cast iron skillets and lanterns; that he had collected over the years.

Reggie drove up to the row of chicken houses on the Murphy's hundred acre farm. This farm had at least fifteen breeding chicken houses. She saw a man coming out of one the houses holding a water hose, she didn't recognize him.

"Hey, I'm detective Memphis, I'm looking for Freddie Jones." The man laid down the hose, and walked towards her jeep. He didn't introduce himself.

"He quit working here last year, he works up at the Port now. He got fired for stealing some money, I assume you are looking for him cause he's done something else?" he said.

"Well, I don't know about that, just have some questions, do you have his cell phone number?"

"No, I don't and don't care to talk to him anymore." Reggie knew Freddie had burned his bridges with people around here because he couldn't be trusted.

"Ok, I understand. Thank you for the information." She rolled up the window as she drove away. The stench of the chicken houses always makes her gag but she has always been told "It's the smell of money."

When Reggie got home that evening she was greeted by her cat, Sammy on the back porch. Sammy was a big male black and white cat that Reggie has had for several years. She inherited him from her neighbors. When the neighbors across the street moved, they left Sammy for her to take care of. They said he liked her better because she fed him and stayed at her house all the time anyway. Sammy had been rescued by a local truck driver who kept seeing him down on the docks along the Savannah River when he made deliveries there. He was a scrawny homeless cat when rescued. The neighbors decided to take care of him and soon he became King Cat of the neighborhood. He used to go from house to house and get fed but always came back to Reggie's to sleep. Now that he is older, he prefers mostly to stay inside Reggie's house. Sammy meowed and clawed at the bag of cat food. She knew he was ready to be fed his evening meal. She kicked off her boots, took off her gun holster, her cowboy hat and set her keys and phone on the kitchen table. She fed Sammy and poured herself some wine. As she was making her way back out to the porch, she heard her phone ringing, What now? she thought.

"Detective Memphis, it's Terrence Jenkins from Chicago," he said as if she wouldn't remember who he was. "Can we meet tomorrow morning? I have some questions."

"Sure, Terrence, Can you meet me at the Country Kitchen for breakfast at 8:30?"

"Yes, that would be great, I have always wanted to try some cheese grits." He laughed. "Call me TJ, everyone does."

"Darlene makes the best grits, you will be hooked. See you then."

Later that evening, she laid awake while Sammy purred at the foot of her bed. She kept thinking that Kendra could be on a trip or choosing not to come home. Has a crime been committed or not? What are the facts right now? She is gone, she hasn't called into work, no one has heard nor seen her. Drug binge? On a vacation with a new boyfriend? Kidnapped? Or worse, murdered?

CHAPTER 2

Kendra didn't know how long she had been on the train. The container car had been pitch black but now she could see a tiny crack of sunlight. The train rumbled down the track, her chest pounding with the fear of what will happen when the train stops. Where was she going? Why had she been taken? The pounding in her head was getting worse, it felt like it was going to explode. She must have been drugged. She remembered the drink and a puncture to her upper arm. Why would he do this? She could feel the tears in her eyes but the rest of her face felt numb. She was laying on a small bed with her hands handcuffed to the bed. Her feet were tied and her mouth was covered with tape. This is a nightmare but I'm awake.

The train whistle was so loud, the vibration of the container car on the tracks was making her headache worse. She could barely move her body and legs. Her stomach was churning, her back was soaked with sweat. As she laid there wondering what was happening, she felt the train slowing down and then it came to stop. Was she going to get out now? Her heart pounded, she could feel her whole body shaking. She could hear loud noises and what sounded like other trains. Where was she? The train was stopped for what seemed like hours. She could hear sounds of trains moving on tracks all around her. All of a sudden, she could feel the container car being lifted up, it was slowly swinging in the air. She began to cry, shaking all over. Was she about to die? The noises were so loud outside. No one could hear her moaning.

She felt the container car being lowered, then a hard landing. After a few minutes, she was moving again but it didn't sound like a train. The train car had been placed on a truck bed. She was being moved by truck. Eventually, she knew the truck would be unloaded, where was it going? What will happen when they stop? She couldn't stop shaking but didn't feel cold, sweat was running down her back. She kept moving her legs and feet trying to loosen the rope tied around her ankles. Her cowboy boots had been taken off but her socks were left on. What was this band on her wrist? She didn't have enough light to see what it looked like but knew it had been put on her wrist while she was passed out. She had to focus on how to survive whatever this was that was happening to her. She closed her eyes to concentrate on the sounds around her. She knew the truck was in traffic, the slowing and stopping movements. It sounded like she was in a city. She could hear car horns and sirens. She could hear loud deep sounding horns that sounded like a ship horn. She had to be close to the ocean.

The truck had stopped but the motor was still running. She could hear a loud noise, like a machine that she had heard before. Once again, she felt the train car being lifted. A crane was lifting it, with deafening beeping noises. This time the landing felt different, Oh my God, she was on a ship. The container car slightly moved up and down with each container being set down beside the container she was trapped in. The ship was being loaded. She had to be in Savannah, Georgia, on the river at the large port. The only port she knows about is Savannah and the travel time made sense to her. It seemed that several hours had passed while she continued to hear and feel the cars being loaded. She could hear voices in the distance when the crane wasn't moving but couldn't hear what was being said. The faint voices were not speaking English. The glimpse of sunlight had gone away and it was pitch black again.

She jerked and opened her eyes when she heard someone trying to open the container door, she must have fallen asleep. Her heart was pounding out of her chest. A man with a flashlight opened the door quickly, climbed in and shut the door behind him with the flashlight blinding her. She couldn't see what he looked like. He took the handcuffs off and handed her a sandwich and bottle of water. Her mouth was still taped. He held a gun to her head, she could feel the barrel pressing against her temple. He took the tape off her mouth, still holding the gun to her head. She sipped the water and threw the sandwich at him. He never spoke. He applied more tape to her mouth and handcuffed her wrists again. He motioned to her and showed her a bucket and toilet paper. He pointed to her. She shook her head no. He picked up the sandwich and left. What was happening to her? Who is he? Why didn't he speak? If this was a kidnapping, her family didn't have any money, why her? She was feeling nauseous and weak with her head still pounding. Tears streamed down her face.

CHAPTER 3

Reggie walked into the restaurant and spotted TJ right away. He looked more casual today. He was wearing a purple Polo shirt, no suit today. As she approached the booth, she heard him say, "You're late but you found the person you were looking for". TJ smiled up at her.

She smiled, "Clever."

Darlene came over to take their order. She smiled at Reggie with a hint of raising her eyebrow as she made eye contact with her.

Reggie pointed to TJ, "Hey Darlene, meet TJ from Chicago. He works for Channel 4 News."

"Reggie, I knew you would be famous one day, is he doing a story about you?"

"Hell no, Darlene, He is here to get to know Birch Creek and try your cheese grits." Reggie stared at him, daring him not to say a word about missing people.

"That's right, I want some cheese grits and toast with honey, oh and coffee, lots of coffee,"

"Coffee and pie for me, whatever kind you have today."

"Pie for breakfast?" TJ asked. She nodded yes.

"Ok, so, what questions do you have?" Reggie asked.

"Well, to start, where can I find the 'Wagon Wheel? I tried to google it but found nothing. I also can't find any news about the 4 missing teens."

Reggie laughed. "I'm going to take you on a tour today but I need you to explain to me what your story will be if you don't have any leads? "Reggie's smile faded as she wanted him to know she was serious.

"I'm an investigative journalist. My job is to find the story and that's what I'll do."

Darlene arrived with the grits, toast and pie. TJ took a bite of the grits.

"Not really sure what I'm eating but it tastes good. Your apple pie looks delicious."

"It is delicious and just what I needed to get my day started."

"Are you thinking there is no story here?" He asked.

"You're the investigative reporter, you tell me. I'll show you around and we can talk then you tell me what you think."

Reggie could feel her face blushing, was she flirting with him?

"If a small town has 5 people now missing, that seems like a story to me. Are you thinking they have been kidnapped? Or do we have some murders taking place?" TJ cocked his head to the side, looking puzzled at Reggie's lack of responsiveness.

"Let's take that tour and I will explain what I know so far."

TJ grabbed both checks, "these are together" he said as he handed Darlene his credit card. "Well, thank you," Reggie looked up at Darlene who once again raised her eyebrow at Reggie. She puckered her lips and smiled at Reggie and hesitated as if she wanted to ask her a question. Darlene had been trying to play matchmaker for Reggie for a while but Reggie never liked any of the ones Darlene had picked. She had her heart broken and she wasn't ready to date anyone.

"I'll meet you outside, you can ride with me." Reggie wanted to smoke before he came outside.

TJ liked Reggie's southern accent. He liked how confident and decisive she seemed. She drives a big jeep, wears a gun and cowboy hat, no wonder I'm intimidated, he thought. As they drove through town, Reggie waved at a few people they passed. Everyone seemed to know her and recognize her.

"See that big arena over there? That is the local Saddle Club. Birch Creek holds an event every year called 'Wagon Train,' it's a week-long event held during the 4th of July week. Riding competitions, races, a parade and an actual wagon train are all part of the events. This brings in people and their horses from all over. Many of the locals camp out right here at the Saddle Club, some sleep in tents, their horse trailers or their wagons."

TJ's eyes widened, "you mean they have actual horse and buggy wagons?"

"Yes, most of the wagons are pulled by strong mules and the horses are used for barrel racing, or other races or shows. It's called Wagon Train, not wagon wheel. There is no place around here called the wagon wheel. Kendra was last seen at Wagon Train before she went missing. It's our busiest week out of the year at the Sheriff's office. Mostly people getting into fights while intoxicated, that sort of thing." Reggie explained.

TJ threw his hands up, "OK, now it's making sense, except it's hard to believe people still own wagons and go on wagon train rides. Birch Creek is like the wild west." Reggie smiled and kept driving.

Reggie drove over to the Little Mountain trailer park. She stopped on the street and pointed to an old blue trailer that looked abandoned. The trailer looked abandoned but the yard had been maintained. She wasn't sure if someone had rented that old place or not.

"Do you see that trailer on the left? Behind it used to be a shed almost as big as the trailer but it blew up when Ms. Doris Bailey was trying to cook her own batch of meth. Doris Bailey is Kendra's aunt who called you. She paid her dues and is doing fine now. She let Kendra move in with her when Kendra's mother kicked her out of the house. Doris knew if she didn't, Kendra was going down the wrong path. Doris is clever, those teens she told you about - they aren't still missing. They were partying up on the mountain and finally came back home. She decided it would get your attention to embellish the truth a little. Obviously, it worked." She stopped and looked over to see TJ's reaction. He was looking straight ahead.

"Son of a bitch," he said. "Is Kendra not missing and on some drug binge in some old wagon somewhere?"

"Possibly" Reggie said as she shrugged her shoulders.

As Reggie drove over to the Elementary School, TJ was quiet staring out the window. She thought he was probably thinking how to tell his boss there may not be any story at all and this trip was a waste of time.

"On Saturdays, the local farmers come over here to the parking lot for a make-shift farmers market. Some of the locals bring their fried pies, homemade soaps, pickled okra, all sorts of homemade items to sell. It's a great place to talk to the locals who know all the gossip in the county. They sit out here for hours and cook barbecue. Tomorrow is Saturday, you should meet the locals." Reggie looked over at TJ. He was looking at his cell phone.

"I'm not sure yet if I am staying. I need to make some calls." As soon as the words came out of his mouth, his phone rang. TJ let it ring a few times, he was hesitating to answer.

"Umm, Hey, I am with Detective Memphis right now. I am familiarizing myself with the town. Let me call you back later, ok?" He knew he didn't want to talk to her and probably wouldn't call back later.

Reggie realized he may not be talking to his boss, is it a wife? Girlfriend? She thought about what she might look like, probably beautiful, young and fit too. She saw him shaking his head as he hung up and put his phone in his pocket.

"I need to talk with Freddie and show you one last landmark." Reggie made a u-turn and headed up to the railroad port.

As they approached the port, TJ said, "wow, I never would have known this was here in Birch Creek." I don't think I have ever seen anything like this. "Huge cranes towered over most of the port area. They were for loading and unloading the cargo containers. Trains were parked being loaded and unloaded. Trucks were coming in and out as Reggie turned in. She had to stop at the guard house before entering.

"Well, hey Michael. Is Freddie Jones working today?" she asked. Michael's face lit up as he looked up and saw Reggie.

"No, Freddie works swing shift, he will be in on Monday. You mean you didn't want to come see me instead?" He smiled.

Reggie laughed, "Is there something I should know?"

"I know you love me Reg, you're just trying to find an excuse to come see me." He winked at her.

"You know it," she said. "If you talk to him, please let him know I'm looking for him." She waved bye and she circled the building to exit the entrance. Reggie had been friends with Michael since elementary school. He always flirted with her but never asked her out.

"I think you've got a fan club, that guy and Darlene at the restaurant." TJ was smiling as he looked up. "Stop, wait a minute, what is that up there?" TJ asked. He saw a man on top of what looked like a grain bin, next to the fence where the trains come into the port.

Reggie looked up, "Oh my goodness, bless his heart, the short story is, that's Mr. McGregor or we all call him Captain Joe. He was in a car accident years ago and suffered some brain damage. He was around 50 years old when the accident happened, and was hit by a drunk driver. The drunk driver died on impact. He was in a coma for a long time and actually had to re-learn how to do everything. He was a successful realtor and a veteran. He hasn't been able to work since but is on a mission to protect the port. He climbs up the side of that Silo all the time and thinks he is the captain watching over the port. His family finally built him a deck around it and some decent stairs since he was going to keep going up there even when they tried to get him to stop. That's a fake gun and no bullets. It gives him something to do. I'm so used to him being up there, I don't even pay attention."

"Wow, he could scare someone who didn't know him," TJ said as he kept looking up and then waved. "That sounds like a story in the making. I bet he scares the hell out of people passing by."

"I guess you are right." She headed back into town.

"Alright, TJ, Let me take you back to your car now. By the way, where are you staying?"

TJ took a deep breath and sighed. His mood had changed.

"I am actually staying about 30 minutes north of Birch Creek, that was the closest hotel. This town needs a hotel."

"Oh, I hadn't even thought about you not staying here in Birch Creek. Well, no easy way to meet up for a drink then." Reggie glanced his way. His eyes got big like he was surprised by what she said.

"I mean it's Friday, relax a little." she said. He looked over at her but stayed quiet until she pulled up next to his rental car.

"I will call you later, I need to work on some things." he said as he was getting out of the jeep.

"Thanks for showing me around. I enjoyed the tour. Your explanation of every-thing has kind of made me rethink my trip."

"I understand."

He got into his car. Reggie lit a cigarette, Damn, I sounded like I was coming on to him, what the hell made me say that?

Sammy was sitting in the window when she arrived at home. Her house was in the small downtown area, a street right behind the courthouse. She bought the house 5 years ago from an old family friend, Ms. Betty, who was moving to Flor-ida to be with her daughter. The house was kept in great shape by Ms. Betty who had it painted again and a new metal roof installed right before selling it. Reggie was proud of herself for being a homeowner on a prime piece of property. She had screened in the back porch since moving in and loves sitting out there in the eve-nings. Sammy especially loves it too. He watches the birds flying by and has a special spot where the sun shines in on the floor where he takes most of his naps. Reggie sat out on the porch to eat her salad and then smoked what she thought would be her last cigarette. She knew it was a bad habit and needed to quit, maybe today would be the day. She grabbed her gummy bears to snack on too, another habit. She heard a car pull up in the driveway, Sammy ran back inside. She opened the screen door, looked out and saw it was Sheriff Johnson. Sheriff Johnson had known Reggie since she was a child. He knew what her childhood had been like with her parents. He was the one who mentored her as she started working for him as a deputy. Birch Creek fell under "the good ole boy" system but he was trying to change that. No one seemed supportive of her moving up as a detective except Sheriff Johnson. He had always told her she had the skills and intellect to figure things out. She faced lots of scrutiny over the years but she never wanted to disappoint Sheriff Johnson, he was the one who believed in her.

"Hey Reggie, we need to talk. I just got word from Mr. Adams that his daugh-ter, Myra, didn't come home last night. She is 16 and always makes curfew. He and his wife have been calling all her friends and been up all night. None of her friends have heard from her nor saw her last night after work. I have Ed at the station work-ing on getting information from the camera's downtown to see what time she left work. She works at Millstone Pizza in town."

"Yes, she's such a sweet girl, always has a smile on her face. Isn't she one of the academic scholars this year?" asked Reggie.

"You are correct, her father said she isn't one to stay out past her curfew, never known her to drink, or anything. Her parents are going to meet us at the station this afternoon."

"Ok, I will see you there in a few minutes." Reggie cleaned up her salad plate and left the house shortly after Sheriff Johnson backed down the driveway. Another girl missing, what is happening? As she drove to the station, she contemplated letting TJ know about this new development but she decided to wait.

Myra's parents were already in the conference room waiting when Reggie walked in. Mrs. Adams looked so tired and her eyes were swollen and red from crying. Mr. Adams started rambling off a list of everyone they had called.

"I'm so sorry you are going through this and it's hard to even know what "this" is. Do me a favor and write down who you talked to already because I will re-interview them and anyone else close to her." She handed Mr. Adams a pen and piece of paper. "Have you talked with the manager and crew at Millstone?"

"No", Mrs. Adams spoke up. "We only have the number for the restaurant, not her boss's personal number. His name is Allen, he is the manager. I tried to call the Millers but didn't reach them", she said.

Reggie knew the Millers very well, they owned Millstone Pizza and she had dated their son, Harris, for a couple of years until she found out he had another girlfriend. She happened to find out the night the girlfriend was actually giving birth to his son. She almost had the baby in his truck on the way to the hospital but EMS got there in time to get her in the ambulance and then the baby was born. Reggie was devastated and heartbroken, she thought he was the one she would marry. A few months after the breakup, she realized she really loved his parents more than him. They were substitutes for her parents who never really cared for her. She misses her relationship with his parents but knew it was all for the best. Thank goodness for unanswered prayers, she thought. Reggie hasn't seen her own parents since her grandmother's funeral when they barely recognized who she was.

"I will try to reach the Millers if the manager isn't available." Reggie explained. "Did Myra mention where she was going after she got off work?"

"She didn't say she was going anywhere, we thought she was coming home." Mr. Adams spoke up. He handed the list back to Reggie.

"Thank you, here is my card, go home, try to rest and I will be back in touch with you. If you hear any news, call me right away." Reggie walked them out of the side door. She turned to walk back to her office when Ed came down the hall.

"We have some camera footage from the parking lot when she left work at 10:00 last night. She was by herself and turned right out of the parking lot. We know she stopped at the Handy Mart. The outside camera wasn't working but the one inside was on. She bought gum and a Yoo Hoo at 10:06. No one was with her. I'm still working on other cameras in the area."

"Alright, thanks, keep me posted. I am going out to do some interviews." Reggie yelled as she walked out the door. She headed over to Millstone Pizza. Allen, the manager, was there. He looked surprised when Reggie shared she was Detective Memphis and needed to talk with him about Myra.

"What about Myra, did something happen?" Allen asked.

"Well, we aren't sure, she didn't come home last night and no one has seen nor heard from her. Did anything out of the ordinary happen while she was working?" Reggie asked as she saw Myra's photo on the wall as "Employee of the Month." Allen sat down at a nearby table.

"We were very busy on Thursday night but nothing unusual happened." Reggie was pacing around the dining area.

"Can you give me a list of everyone who worked last night with her and possibly which customers she had?" Reggie handed him her notepad and pen.

"I can give you the list of who worked last night, right now but the customers will take a little longer, it will only be ones who used a debit or credit card but you are welcomed to look at the video from the cameras." Allen said as he started writing down a list with phone numbers included.

"Ed from the Sheriff's dept. will come over to view the video, he is the expert." Reggie thanked the manager for his cooperation and the contact information and left. She wanted a cigarette as she started up her jeep but grabbed the gummy bears instead. She could feel her neck and shoulders tightening up. Kendra may really be missing along with Myra. She called Ms. Doris Bailey.

"Hey, it's Detective Memphis, Have you heard from Kendra or heard anything else?

"No, I haven't heard from her. I just know something is wrong, this isn't like her. I did hear that Freddie told his aunt that he heard she may have gotten arrested", Doris said. Reggie rolled her eyes.

"I would know if she had gotten arrested and I would have called you first thing, I really need to talk with Freddie who seems to be the only one with any news. Please get his cell number from his aunt if you don't mind and call me when you get it." Doris agreed to call right away and get his number. "Also," Reggie added, "all the local area hospitals have been checked for anyone matching Kendra's description. No leads."

"Thank you Regina, I will text you his phone number."

As she arrived back at her office, Doris texted Reggie Freddie's cell phone number. She called him right away. When he answered she could hear some loud noises in the background and it sounded like he was outside.

"Freddie, It's Detective Memphis. I hear you have some information about Kendra. I need you to come to the station to talk with me this afternoon."

"Umm, ok. Not sure I know much of anything but I can come by. I'm up here at the lumber yard but I can leave in a few minutes."

"That will be great, see you in a few minutes." Reggie knew Freddie and his brothers who owned the lumber yard. His brothers were older and they were in business together. They called it the Lumber yard but it was more of a logging business. His brothers were known to be big spenders and flaunted money all over town. Reggie had always heard that they were crooked in their business dealings but no charges were ever made against them. They were either obeying the law or really good at hiding their criminal activity. She understood why they didn't let Freddie be a part of their business. Freddie had a reputation of not being honest. He had stolen anything he could get his hands on, he had some addiction problems and a hot temper. When Doris had mentioned him the first time, Reggie was thinking he isn't the best witness to be giving details. He could never be a character witness for anyone.

CHAPTER 4

"Shit, I have to go talk with the detective." Phil, his brother, asked, "What about?"

"She wants to ask me questions about Kendra. Says she heard that I have some information." He was wiping the sweat off his head with his t-shirt.

"Don't fuck it up like you always do" Phil was shaking his head. "You don't think she knows about anything else do you?" he was walking closer to Freddie pointing his finger.

"No, she just wants to ask questions about Kendra." Freddie stepped back. Still pointing his finger, "you better be right."

Freddie was feeling nauseous. His (half) brothers always blame him for what his father did. Freddie was only 8 when his father left him and his mother and his 2 half brothers. He took all of their money and left them with nothing. His mother had received an inheritance from her parents and he took it. Freddie never knew how much money his father took from them. He has never been found. His half brother's father had money but only gave money at Christmas and birthdays to Phil and Simon, never giving it to their mother. Freddie's dad was hooked on pills and methamphetamine. Freddie doesn't know if he is dead or alive. Phil and Simon always say he is just like his dad and won't be anything but a drug addict too.

Freddie sat in his car thinking about what he was going to say. I saw her at the fireworks, she was drunk and with some guy that I didn't know, that's what he would say. Freddie was tapping his finger on the console, he rolled a joint. I need to settle my nerves before I go talk to her. He drove home, smoked and then took a shower to rinse the smell. I have to stay calm, not give up any information. I wonder where Kendra is right now? Is she ok? His nausea was getting worse.

Freddie arrived about two hours after speaking to Reggie on the phone. She walked him into her office to ask him some questions.

"Tell me about seeing Kendra at the fireworks."

When Freddie started to talk, Ed stuck his head in the door and said, "oh excuse me, I didn't know you had anyone in here." He looked at Freddie and motioned for Reggie to step out into the hall.

"Who is that?"

"It's Freddie Jones, I am asking him questions about seeing Kendra at the fireworks."

"I recognized his face from the video at Millstone's last night. He was there. He was a customer of Myra's and he was drinking a pitcher of beer in the video."

Reggie was clenching her jaw, feeling her neck tightening.

"Let me move him to the interview room and record the interview." she said as she opened the door.

"Freddie, Let's move into the interview room to do an official interview because I have learned some new information. Follow me." she said sternly.

Freddie threw his hands up and followed her.

She sat across from Freddie and explained this interview was being recorded and started right in asking questions.

"I understand that you saw Kendra the last night of Wagon Train at the fireworks, is this correct?"

"Yes, I saw her, she was drunk and hanging on to some guy who I didn't know."

"Was she with anyone else, did you speak to her? Did you see her leave, can you describe this guy who she was with?"

Reggie purposefully spewed off several questions at once to him.

"Hell, slow down and let me answer you. She was with a group of maybe 4 or 5 people who I didn't know. The guy had dark hair and was tatted up. What else did you ask me?"

"I asked if you saw her leave and did you talk to her? Also, can you describe any of his tattoos?" Reggie asked as she was making notes.

"No, I didn't see her leave and no, I didn't get a close look at him, just saw he had both arms with sleeve tattoos." Freddie was looking a bit frustrated.

"Did you talk to her?"

"No, I didn't" he was rubbing his temples at this point.

"Freddie, you were at Millstone last night. Can you tell me anything that happened?" "What the hell, how do you know I was at Millstones, why all these questions?' He was getting red faced, "are you following me?"

"No, not following you but you were on video footage. We may have another missing girl, this time a 16 year old who happened to be your waitress last night. Did you notice anything about her or anyone else last night?" Reggie slowed down with the questions.

"Another missing girl, shit!" he said. "Umm. no, there were a lot of people there last night, I ate and then left." he was looking down picking at a scratch on his hand.

"Do you remember what time you left?"

"No idea, look at your video footage." he cocked his head to one side.

"Tell me this, why did you say Kendra could be in jail?" Reggie was clenching her jaw again because she knew he was not telling the truth.

"I said she might be because she was drunk and that guy looked shady, that's all I know.

Can I go now?"

"How did you get the scratch on your hand, Freddie?" Freddie looked down at his hand.

"I got it from loading logs onto a truck." "Oh, you work for your brothers, now?"

"No, I was up there and just helped out. Can I go now?"

"You seem to be getting very defensive, Freddie, why is that?"

"I'm getting pissed because you seem to be questioning me like I did something bad. Can I go?"

"Sure, here is my card, call me if you think of anything else." Reggie said as she opened the interview room door. She walked him out and then asked Ed to see what time Freddie left Millstone last night and see if there was any video footage of him leaving and where he may have gone afterwards.

"I don't trust him. Also, can you track both girls' cell phones and their social media accounts?"

"I'm already working on all of it and I will look at Freddie's actions last night," Ed said.

Freddie was sweating, nauseous and still high. He tried to call Rum. No answer as usual, he thought. He wanted to know that Kendra was doing ok, Why had he followed through with it? He needed to check on Myra - he had refused to help with her disappearance. Woody and Domino had gotten him involved with this crazy maniac, Rum. They told him he would make lots of money working for him but he didn't know how much control the maniac would have over him. This was wrong.

He met Woody and Domino a few years ago when he was put in jail in Florida. He robbed a liquor store and got caught just as he ran out the back door. Woody and Domino were two characters that immediately became friends of Freddie's. They made fun of his southern accent but were always trying to talk like him. They were the only two people that he ever thought of as friends. It was so surprising when they came to Birch Creek to stay at Rum's house, their new boss. That's when Freddie met Rum.

CHAPTER 5

Reggie's cell phone rang, It was Mr. Adams. "Any news yet about our daughter?" He asked.

"We are working on it, we know she left work at 10pm and then stopped at the handy mart to buy some gum and a drink. We are searching for her car too. We are reviewing the video from the restaurant and I have talked with her manager. I will let you know more as we figure this out."

"Her cell phone goes straight to voicemail and none of her friends have heard from her." He said.

"We are working on tracking her cell phone too." Reggie explained. "I will be in touch."

Reggie walked outside to smoke and think about the facts so far. She got a text from TJ.

"Can we have that drink?" It read. *"I am going back to Chicago in the morning."* *"Yes, come by my house, I'm tired and need to unwind."* She sent him her address. *"7:30 ish?"* She typed.

"Ok" he responded.

What is wrong with me, I just invited him to my house, she thought.

When she got home, she realized how tired she was, it must be the stress of this case. Her body seemed to hurt all over. She needed a hot shower.

After she cleaned up her house and herself, she heard a car in the driveway. She peeked out the back door of the porch. TJ looked different tonight, a t-shirt and basketball shorts. She liked his casual look too.

"Hey, I'm back here on the porch, come join me." Reggie yelled. As he entered the screen door, Sammy raised his head and looked but then went back to sleep.

"That's Sammy," she pointed over to him.

"NIce to meet you Sammy," he laughed. Reggie was more casual that night too. She had showered, let her hair air dry and had on a T-shirt dress and was barefooted. She put on a little makeup but she wasn't really sure why. She had always been complimented on how pretty she was just being natural. She had an olive complexion and tanned easily. Her strawberry blonde hair and blue eyes came from her dad's side of the family.

"So, what's your poison? I have beer, wine, gin or bourbon?" she raised her eyebrow in question.

"I'm not a beer drinker, but I love bourbon." He said.

"Bourbon it is and I'll have one too," she smiled. They sat down on her cushioned chairs on the back porch taking slow sips of the bourbon on ice.

"I'm leaving in the morning, back to the grind in Chicago. No story here so I can't justify staying."

"I thought you were going to find a story?" She then hesitated but said, "Well, not so fast, we have another missing girl." Reggie explained. "She is 16 and didn't come home last night and not one to be out partying, a very responsible young scholar. I have been working on it all day."

"Why didn't you start with that?" he asked. "Do you think it's related to Kendra missing?" "We don't know yet, but I have a suspicion that Freddie Jones knows more than what he is telling me."

"Wait, is he the one who saw Kendra and works at that train port?" TJ sat up in his chair leaning forward.

"Yes, he is. He also happened to be served last night by the missing 16 year old at

Millstone's pizza. He is not the best witness nor is he trustworthy, I got him a little rattled today and I plan to increase the pressure too."

TJ looked intrigued and asked, "Can I have another?" As he was holding up his glass.

"Yes, I got some snacks, we can eat inside and have another drink, too. Come on in and I will make it for us."

"Your house is really nice", he called out to her from the living room. She had a swinging door in the kitchen that joined her living room. She kept it propped open all the time so Sammy could go in and out. The house was old but had character, built in bookcases in the living room and a built-in cabinet in the kitchen.

"I love it, it's mine and mine alone." She set down a tray of fruit, cheese and some crackers on the coffee table.

"Here you go, enjoy,"

"Have you ever been married?" he asked.

That's a random question for him to be asking, she thought. "No, and you?"

"Yes, I'm married. It's been about 2 years."

Damn, of course he is married. She was trying not to show disappointment on her face. "Oh, any kids?" Reggie asked.

"No, we don't plan to have any."

Reggie was thinking why not but didn't want to pry. "Can I ask your age?" he asked.

Another random question again.

"Don't you know not to ask a woman her age?" She tried to look serious but couldn't hold back a smile.

"Just kidding, I'm 35 and you?" she responded.

"I'm 34, Wow, you look great, I would have guessed 29."

"Oh, the bourbon makes you a charmer, I see." she laughed.

"I'm serious," he said. She was thinking he is probably full of shit.

"Ok, Thank you, I will accept that compliment. Since you started this 20 questions conversation, I have one for you. Were you an athlete in high school or college.?"

"Yes, football and basketball in high school then basketball in college. What about you?" Reggie took a sip of her drink and answered.

"When I was in highschool, I was part of the rodeo circuit. Barrel racing."

"I'm a black man from Chicago, not sure I know what barrel racing is." he took a sip and waited for her response.

"It's a timed competition where you ride your horse around 3 different barrels as fast as you can without knocking over the barrels. I was pretty good at it back in the day." She laughed.

"I'm going to google it and check it out," he said.

"I have a video on my phone. My friend Janice sent it to me the other day. It's the 2 of us at the state competition." She scooted over close to show him the video. She could smell his cologne. It smelled so good, she thought.

"Well, look at you cowgirl, that's impressive!" He stared at her for a few seconds until his phone vibrated.

He looked at his phone, stood up.

"Do you mind if I use your bathroom?"

"Of course not, down the hall to your right." Reggie said as she couldn't shake the feeling she got when he stared at her. It gave her some butterflies and a feeling she hadn't felt in a long time. I might be a little tipsy, she thought.

"I need to go, early flight. If the missing girls aren't found soon and you think crimes are being committed, let me know and I'll be back." he said as he took his glass into the kitchen. Reggie followed him, taking the glass from his hand.

"It's been great meeting you Regina Memphis." he said as he stared at her again. She felt like a shy little girl all of a sudden. He reached around to hug her.

"Keep in touch," he said.

"Alright, you too." Reggie said as Sammy meowed.

"Bye, Sammy, nice to meet you too. "He waved at Reggie as he left out the screened back door.

"What the hell was that?" she thought to herself. She went out on the porch and lit up a cigarette. "He is married, he is married," she kept saying over and over to herself.

TJ left knowing he really wanted to stay longer and get to know this beautiful southern woman. He had never met anyone like her and he was intrigued. His thoughts led back to his text message. He needed to go back to Chicago and confront this issue. The truth has been confirmed.

CHAPTER 6

Reggie woke up early on Saturday morning ready to focus on these investigations, she was sure TJ was on his way back to Chicago by now. She wanted to check in with Ed on the video cameras, cell phone and social media tracking and what time Freddie left Millstone Pizza. On her way to the office, she stopped at the Handy Mart.

"Good Morning, Natalie, How's it going?"

"Hey Detective Memphis, I'm doing well, getting used to this small town. I must say everyone has been really nice to me." Natalie smiled.

"I'm sure you are meeting a lot of people who come in here. This is the most popular store in the county. I know Ed from the Sheriff's office obtained some camera footage from here. Were you working on Thursday night?" Reggie asked her as she grabbed her bag of gummy bears. "Yes, I told Ed that I remember that girl coming in, she was very polite and I had seen her a couple of times. I reported to the manager that the camera outside must be broken. It had been working before that night."

"Hmm, that's interesting, I'm sure Ed is checking it all out." Reggie gave her money for the gummy bears and thanked her for the information. Reggie wanted to make sure she told Ed the outside camera quit working right before Myra disappeared.

Sheriff Johnson was standing outside when Reggie arrived at the office. "The Adams think we are not moving fast enough on this investigation."

"I understand they are worried and upset but technically we actually started earlier than we should have on it, Myra had only been missing or whereabouts unknown for less than 12 hours." Reggie snapped back.

"I am feeling the pressure too." Reggie said.

"We need to make an official statement on this. Let's meet with Ed and see what we have so far." Sheriff Johnson announced. Reggie nodded in agreement. Ed walked into Sheriff Johnson's office with a file folder in his hand.

"I just got back the information on their social media and cell phones and I have combed through all of it. Neither female has been on social media since they were missing. I also don't see any leads like new boyfriends or anybody tracking them. BUT, here's something that ties them together. Both females' cell phones last pinged off of the same cell tower location with no more activity on each night they went missing. I know it was at different times and dates, but I think both girls or both cell phones were in the same location, I think we got a lead here." He said as he smiled at Reggie.

"Great work, Ed." Sheriff Johnson replied.

"Yes, this is a lead. Now tell me the location," Reggie jumped up.

"Let me show you on the GPS - Both cell phones stopped working within about 50 yards of each other. This area is wooded," Ed explained.

"Wait, that is the wetlands area, owned by the Department of Natural Resources. We need search teams going out ASAP." Reggie raised her voice knowing this is a good lead.

"Let me call together a search party," Sheriff Johnson said.

Ed spoke up to say, "You may have to go public soon." The sheriff shook his head yes in acknowledgment.

"I need to notify the families that we are forming a search party but emphasize it could just be looking for cell phones. I don't want to give them false hope." Reggie said.

Reggie made the phone calls. She knew this would lead to Sheriff Johnson holding a press conference this afternoon when word spreads.

She texted TJ. The text read: *We have a lead that ties the 2 missing girls cases together, well sort of. The Sheriff will hold a press conference this afternoon.* She stuck to the facts and hit send.

She drove out to the wetlands. It was only 5 miles from the Sheriff's office. She wanted to get there first to get ready for search and rescue teams.

As soon as she parked her jeep, it started raining. Damn, we don't need rain right now, this area will flood, she thought to herself. She stayed in her jeep waiting on the rain to slack up, it kept raining, no one had arrived yet and she had been there at least 30 minutes. Also, no response from TJ as she looked at her phone.

Ed called her as she waited.

"Freddie left Millstones at 9:55. He turned left and no more camera footage after he left downtown, at least I haven't found any more cameras in the area yet."

"Thanks Ed, I appreciate all you do."

She hung up and retrieved her gummy bears instead of cigarettes. She could now hear the helicopter overhead so she knew it wouldn't be long before everyone arrived. The search and rescue teams assembled along with several volunteers, family and friends. Already, there must have been at least 50 people and Reggie knew more would be arriving. Sheriff Johnson arrived too and wanted to be on the scene in case there was any breaking news. Reggie was fascinated regarding the way the search and rescue teams coordinated everything and were so comforting to the families and friends. Doris Bailey brought Kendra's mother with her because she now believed something had happened to her daughter. Myra's mother was trying to hold back tears but kept wiping her eyes with a tissue. Myra's father was walking around and asking each rescue team member questions. The rain kept coming but that didn't seem to stop their efforts. With the rain came flooding so they could only search around the perimeter until the water level decreased. They would probably have their search and rescue teams out for days on land and in boats in the wetland marshes due to the area being about 5 square miles. Doing the math in her head, Reggie realized this was about 5000 acres. They had somewhat pinpointed the area but with it being wetlands and now flooding, a wider area, possibly the whole area would need to be searched. The locals showed up to help feed the volunteers. They made sandwiches and The Millers brought several pizzas. When it got dark, most of the volunteers were instructed to go home. The rescue team stayed and continued the search.

Sheriff Johnson asked the families and friends to leave and meet him at the sheriff's office in 30 minutes. He would make an official statement and describe the search that is underway. He wanted anyone who might have information to come forward. Reggie stayed at the site until 10PM hoping the rescue dogs would find something. Nothing was found and then the team leader explained that the rain and flooding is making it difficult. The team will stay through the night and a new team will come back in the morning hoping the water level will have decreased by then. She called Sheriff Johnson.

"Sheriff Johnson, I'm going to stay out here at the Wetlands in case they find something." "Reggie, the rescue teams will call me if they find anything. Go home and get some rest. I need you to be rested and alert tomorrow. We have some long days ahead of us."

Reggie reluctantly went home. She knew she needed rest but couldn't sleep. She checked her cell phone. No text or missed call from TJ. It had been such a busy day and she played all the scenes of the day over and over in her head. It was obvious the girls' cell phones had been dumped out at the wetlands but where were Kendra and Myra? She hated to think about this possibly being a homicide. If bodies are out there, those dogs will find them. She couldn't understand why this was happening and what was the motive? She knew pieces to this mysterious puzzle were missing.

CHAPTER 7

She woke up early and noticed it was no longer raining. She knew it would be another long day but thankful the rain stopped. She wondered if Ed had found any more camera footage, she would check with him later. She showered, fed Sammy, and cooked some eggs for an egg sandwich. She resisted the urge to smoke, "today would be the day she quits." On her way to the wetland site, she stopped in at the Handy Mart. Tony was working this morning, he was the manager who usually worked the afternoon shift.

"We have someone coming tomorrow to fix the outside video camera,"

"Yes, Natalie told me she had reported it to you. I like her, I thought she would be here this morning."

"She was supposed to be here, she didn't show up. Eric called me when his shift was ending to say she wasn't here. Eric and I both tried to call her, no answer. She probably overslept, she has been working some double shifts, apparently saving up for a car. You want your pack of Marlboro lights?" he asked.

"No, I have to quit that bad habit." Reggie said but it wasn't a convincing statement even to her. She sighed and grabbed a coffee and diet coke.

"I hope Natalie isn't going to quit this job, I like her and she seemed to enjoy it too." Reggie said.

"I heard about the search, have they found anything?"

"No, but I am hopeful today will be a better day to search. See ya later, "Reggie waved goodbye.

When she arrived at the site, there was already lots of action going on - The dogs were out, there was an air boat heading through the marsh. Volunteers and rescue teams were strategizing to cover the area. There was also a canopy tent set up with the smell of sausage cooking. The community comes together when needed. She felt proud to be a part of Birch Creek's community.

After a few minutes of Reggie talking with the team leader, Sheriff Johnson called her to come into the station.

He wanted to discuss the next steps to take. He said Ed was checking video footage but it was very limited due to not many cameras on the way out to the Wetlands.

She walked into the office, Sheriff Johnson was there with Ed.

"We wanted you to see this video footage from the highway out to the wetlands, It's from the appliance factory entrance camera," Ed said to Reggie.

"Do we have something?" "Maybe," Ed said.

"Look at this truck, I can't make out the year yet but I know it's a Ford. I also can't see the person driving because it's at night but it is on both nights these girls went missing. It is going towards the wetlands and then comes back in just a few minutes. "

"This is something!" Reggie said with excitement in her voice.

"I wonder how many white Ford trucks there are around?" she questioned. "A shitload", Sheriff Johnson, replied.

"I tried to reach the head of security at the GE appliance but he won't be back until tomorrow.

I am hoping he can tell us if that's a regular truck he sees traveling the highway out there and see if he can tell me any more information. I will meet with him first thing in the morning." Ed said.

"Thank you Ed, great work! As usual." Reggie reached over and hugged him. Ed's face turned red as he looked up at Reggie.

"How many people do we know in Birch Creek that drive a white Ford truck.?" Reggie asked.

"Again, a shit load" said Sheriff Johnson.

"I can think of 5 right now off the top of my head," he said.

"I know, it's like a needle in a haystack." Reggie said. "I'm going to go find Freddie again and ask him more questions." Reggie said as she walked out the door.

Reggie drove up to Freddie's brother's logging/lumber yard. She heard shots being fired as she climbed out of the jeep. She carefully walked down the hill, her hand on her gun ready to retrieve it if necessary. Simon and Phil were target practicing. As she walked up announcing herself behind them, she saw their guns.

"Whoa, where did you get those?" They were both holding identical Kimber 1911 45 caliber guns. Reggie knew those were expensive and highly sought after.

"We'll never tell," Simon yelled as he took out his ear plugs.

"We got a good deal on these. Sounds like you know about guns." He said. "What can we do for you Detective Memphis?" Phil asked.

"Have you seen Freddie?"

"Not since he came by bragging about his new truck. Not sure how he affords it" Simon said. "What kind of truck?"

"It's a Silver Toyota Tacoma", Phil spoke up.

"What did he drive before this new truck?" Reggie asked as she was looking at the other guns they had laid out on the bed of their truck. They have a lot of expensive guns, she thought.

"He had a Nissan Sentra." Phil answered. Phil pointed at the guns,

"These are all registered to us and we have the sales slips for them, just in case you were wondering."

Reggie knew they had money and liked to flaunt their wealth.

"Alright, thanks. I need to talk with Freddie, I have some questions. Where does he live?" Reggie asked as she started walking towards her jeep.

"He lives in a trailer right before you get to the Port. It's the only one on a small lot "Simon answered.

Reggie drove up to the trailer they had described. No truck in the driveway but she decided to knock anyway. No answer but she could hear a loud bark inside. She slid her card in the door so he would know she had been there.

She drove back to the Wetlands. More volunteers had shown up when she arrived. She walked over to talk with Joey, the leader of the rescue team.

"We found a ball cap, an old fishing rod and that's it, besides some trash. We will have the cap and fishing rod analyzed even though I don't think either item has anything to do with this search." he said.

"I appreciate everything you guys are doing. I know you will keep me posted."

Reggie went over to talk with the volunteers who were cooking and preparing food. She wanted to ask if any of them were at the fireworks that night or could give her any other information.

She recognized Mrs. Wallace first. Mrs. Wallace had been Reggie's high school Spanish teacher. She was a sweet lady but her class was hard as hell. She expected her students to be fluent in Spanish by the end of the year, which didn't happen.

"Hey, Mrs. Wallace, thank you so much for coming out here to help."

"I am happy to help, I taught both Kendra and Myra, such sweet girls, this is the least I can do."

"Did you happen to attend the fireworks during Wagon Train this year?"

"Yes, several of us teachers got together to go. It was a really good display this year, which must have cost the county a good sum of money," she said.

"Do you remember seeing Kendra that night?"

"No, I didn't but I know that is the night she went missing. Sarah said she saw her before the fireworks. Sarah is here helping with the search, She should be back soon."

"Sarah as in Mrs. Bowen, the English teacher?" Reggie asked. "Yes, she and her husband are here helping to search,"

"Thank you, can you give her my card and ask her to call me in case I miss her today?" "Of course, I will." Mrs. Wallace started handing out sandwiches to the rescue team who was being relieved at this time.

Reggie felt her phone vibrate in her pocket. She pulled her phone out, it was a text from TJ. *"Hey, I'm waiting for clearance to come back to Birch Creek. My boss wants to make sure we have a real story, this time."* the text read. She will text him back later, she decided. She waited for a while and talked to several volunteers. As she started to leave, she saw Mr. and Mrs. Bowen walking up to her.

"Hey Regina, Mrs. Wallace said you wanted to talk to me."

"Yes, first, thank you both for coming out to help. Mrs. Wallace said you remembered seeing Kendra the night of the fireworks?"

"Yes, I said hello to her as we were walking back from the concession stand. We talked for a few minutes. She told me she was working at a flooring business and loved her job." Mrs. Bowen said.

"Was she with anyone? Did she seem intoxicated or anything?" Reggie asked.

"No, not at all, she didn't seem to be under the influence, I remember she was holding a blue slushie that they sell at the concession stand. She did mention that she was waiting on someone but didn't say who." Mrs. Bowen answered. "Do you remember seeing her after you spoke to her?" "No, not after we spoke."

"Alright, thank you for the information. It was great seeing you both, if you happen to remember anything else, please give me a call." Reggie said as she hugged Mrs. Bowen. She had been one of her favorite teachers in school.

"Of course," Mrs. Bowen answered as she hugged Reggie back.

Reggie drove back to her house to eat and check on Sammy even though she knew Sammy didn't need checking on. She walked to the backyard to look at her garden, she picked the watermelon that was good and ripe. She entered through the back porch. Sammy was asleep on her bed when she walked by her room. Reggie ate a salad and cut up the watermelon to eat later. She liked it really cold, so she put it in the refrigerator. She went out on the back porch, the urge was too strong, she lit a cigarette. She justified it to herself by thinking about the pressure and stress of these cases. She inhaled slowly enjoying it. She grabbed her phone and decided to text TJ back. She read his text again.

"I hope you get clearance", she typed. No, that sounds stupid she thought to herself. She deleted it. *"It's definitely a developing story.* "she typed and sent. Short and simple, she thought. As she was contemplating what he might say back to her, her phone rang, it was dispatch.

"This is Detective Memphis." she answered.

"Hey, I need to patch Tony from the Handy mart through to you", the dispatch operator said. "Detective Memphis, this is Tony. We never did hear from Natalie. I called her brother Nate who was listed as her emergency contact. He said he talked to her last night and she mentioned she had to be at work early this morning. Nate, is now on his way from Nashville, he has a feeling something is very wrong." Tony explained.

"Do you have Natalie's address or know where she lives?"

"Yes, she lives in the Hillside apartments about a mile and ½ up on the hill behind the Handy Mart. She walks to work most of the time."

"What's the apartment number?" "It's number 18."

"I will have a deputy meet me at her apartment, I will be in touch. You can call me on my cell number so you don't have to go through dispatch. Also can you text me her brother's contact information?" Reggie asked as she was grabbing her keys to head out the door.

"Yes, sending it now." Tony said.

"Thanks, talk to you soon." Reggie said as she was already in her jeep backing out of the driveway.

Reggie called Sheriff Johnson to make him aware. He would contact dispatch to make sure a deputy meets her at the apartment and get in touch with the landlord to open her apartment if needed. Reggie was thankful for his assistance. He didn't ask questions, he knew she needed help right away.

She arrived at the Hillside apartments which was a newer complex in the area. She immediately saw 2 deputy cars parked in front of apartment 18. They were knocking on the door. As Reggie climbed out of her jeep, a red truck pulled up. Mr. Brown introduced himself as the maintenance man. After 5 minutes of knocking with no answer and hearing no noise inside,

Mr. Brown was able to unlock the door. The deputies entered Natalie's apartment. It was clean and Natalie was obviously not there and nothing looked out of place. They combed through the apartment not finding any signs of any trouble. Maybe she needed time off since she had been working so hard, Reggie tried to reason a legitimate excuse for her not to be around. Reggie asked the deputies to help her talk with the neighbors to see if they saw anything. As they knocked on doors and asked neighbors questions, one of the deputies motioned for Reggie to come over to where he was talking to the next door neighbor, Mr. Sanford. He described seeing Natalie early this morning, when he was taking his trash out. He spoke to her and she said she was on her way to work. He offered to drive her down the hill but she declined. She wanted to get her exercise. He said that was at 7am.

Reggie thanked him for the information and felt sick to her stomach, this is #3 missing.

She called Sheriff Johnson and explained what they knew so far. The sheriff would ask Ed to obtain any camera footage he could get. Reggie immediately thought about the outside camera at Handy Mart not working, damn!, she thought. It was going to be fixed tomorrow.

Reggie went down to the store. She walked in and saw Tony and another cashier talking at the counter. She explained that Natalie wasn't home but heard she left at 7am this morning walking to work. Tony let out a big sigh.

"oh no! Not another one!"

"Do you know what time her brother would be arriving?" Reggie asked. "Not sure."

Reggie went outside to call Natalie's brother.

"Hi, Nate, this is Detective Memphis. Tony said you were on your way here to Birch Creek?" She posed it as a question.

"Yes, I'm about an hour away. This is not like Natalie to not show up at work, I know something is wrong. She is always responsible and would have called if she couldn't make it to work." He started crying while talking to Reggie. "She is my twin sister and I can feel it, something isn't right."

"Tell me what she said last night when you talked to her, please."

"It was the usual, she talked about working lots of hours and saving up her money. She talked about how beautiful the scenery is in Birch Creek and how nice everyone is. I told her I would come visit next weekend and she was thrilled to hear it. She then said shewas tired and had to get up early. That was all we talked about."

"Her neighbor, Mr. Sanford, said she was walking to work this morning. He offered her a ride but she declined." Reggie could hear Nate crying.

"We have deputies out looking for her and also we are gathering all video footage in the area," she added.

"Please let them find her", he said. Reggie knew that he was more than likely unaware of the 2 other girls who were missing.

"I certainly hope we will. Call me if you hear from her. Where are you staying?" Reggie asked.

"I will be at her apartment, she gave me a key already," Nate answered. "I want to be there when she comes back home,"

"Alright, call me if you have questions." Reggie said.

Reggie went back to her office, she sat in the dark for a few minutes to think. She knew something was wrong too. Three females have disappeared now! She has to find them. This can't continue under her watch. Ed texted her to let her know he was gathering the camera footage, cell phone and social media information again. He hoped to have the information back by tomorrow. Reggie was going home to wait for the deputies to call her if they found anything. She lit up a cigarette as soon as she drove out of the parking lot. She needed to calm herself down and hold it together. This was not the day to quit smoking.

When she got home, she sat out on the screened porch, listened to the crickets and frogs while she sipped her wine. Sammy joined her. She felt guilty sitting on her porch smoking and drinking wine when 3 girls were missing. She would meet with Ed in the morning and go back up to the port because Freddie will be back at work.

Her cell phone vibrated, It was TJ texting her.

"Hey cowgirl, I will be coming back to Birch Creek. I will see you when I get there." He typed.

She was too exhausted and too emotional to have a conversation.

"Ok."

CHAPTER 8

It was early Monday morning, She didn't sleep well and got up earlier than usual. When she stepped outside, the heat felt thick and hot.

"It's a hot one today, Sammy," she said as she looked back at him on the porch. She was checking her garden. She picked the ripe tomatoes and squash, took them into the kitchen, washed them in the sink and left them drying. She would stop at Darlene's Country Kitchen to get some pie to go. She was anxious to meet with Ed to see if he had any information for her.

She walked in the conference room at the Sheriff's department with 2 pieces of apple pie, one for her and one for Ed.

"Here you go, Ed." She said as she sat down next to him with the pieces of Darlene's homemade delicious apple pie.

"Just what I needed this morning, thank you." Ed said as he smiled at Reggie.

"I haven't received the cell phone information yet. Social media doesn't show any activity for several days. Camera footage shows her walking out of the complex entrance at 7:06AM. She walks down the hill out of sight. I have a deputy checking on a camera at a house down the hill. So far, the residents haven't been home."

"Well, that tells us she made it out of the apartment complex. What happened between the entrance and the store?" She said out loud. "She was kidnapped. If she had been hit by a car, we would have seen some sort of evidence. She could have been hit and then the person panicked and grabbed her or she was abducted and it was planned." She kept rambling theories out loud. Sheriff Johnson came in and sat down. Ed told him what we know so far.

"Sheriff Johnson, I need some help on this. There is an investigative reporter coming from Chicago who can help me. He can get some of the story out to the public which helps make people come forward with information." Reggie pleaded.

"Ok, I just need him to stick to the facts, no sensationalizing the story." He said.

"I think he will be a big help, which is what I need. Once he gets to town, I think it may be time to hold another press conference." Reggie advised.

"We need to let the public know that another girl seems to be missing."

Reggie was trying to prioritize everything she needed to do for each girl's case. She wanted to go talk to Freddie again at work. She knew they needed to follow up regarding the white Ford truck and talk with many others. She was stressed and wanted to smoke. She walked outside and pulled out her cigarettes. Her phone rang. It was Shay, Kendra's friend.

"Hello Detective Memphis, this is Shay. I have to tell you something that doesn't make sense. My sister saw Kendra at the fireworks. She said she talked to her and she was with Freddie."

"Freddie?" Reggie asked.

"Yes, I asked if she was with anybody else. She said she never saw her with anyone else, just Freddie." Shay said. "Oh, I also asked if she seemed drunk and she said No.

This all seems weird because Freddie is telling a different story. Why would he lie about being with her? He knows more than he is saying, he can't be trusted. It makes me sick to think Freddie may have something to do with this." Shay's voice was escalating. "That asshole lies all the time."

"I may need to interview your sister, I will be back in touch if needed.

Thank you so much for calling me Shay, much appreciated." Reggie said as she hung up the phone.

She got in her jeep to go visit Freddie at work. As soon as she got out of the city limits her phone rang. Ed told her to come back, he just got cell phone information for Natalie's phone and she needed to come back now. Reggie turned around to head back. She knew this was serious if he was calling her to come back immediately.

She walked in to see Ed and Sheriff Johnson looking at the computer screen.

"Reggie, look at this, GPS shows Natalie's phone at the Handy Mart right now and it's still active."

"Do you think she has come back or is it just her phone there or what the hell? Reggie blurted out. I need a deputy to go with me over there ASAP."

Deputy Stone was waiting for her outside in the parking lot, "Ride with me," he said.

Reggie was glad it was Stone, she knew he could handle whatever they were walking into at the store.

As they walked into the Handy Mart, Tony, the store manager and Eric were up front at the counter.

"Tony, have you heard from Natalie?" "No, we haven't." He replied.

"Her cell phone is here and we need to search the premises" , she said sternly.

"What? Her cell phone is here? Of course go ahead and search." He responded with a questionable look as he looked over at Eric. Reggie dialed Natalie's number, they couldn't hear a ring tone. She dialed again and again. Deputy Stone started searching and called for back-up to help. Reggie started asking Eric questions. She turned towards Eric.

"Do you have Natalie's cell phone? Why would it be here?"

"I don't know why her cell is here, I don't know anything about it. I haven't seen it." He was raising his voice in frustration from the questions.

Backup arrived at the back of the building. It was Deputy Lowe and he started yelling for us to come out back.

"I heard something, look up there on the roof. It's a cell phone." As he pointed up on the roof, they could see it. It was on the lower part of the roof above the back doorway, almost hidden by the tree limb that was overgrown and protruding onto the roof. Tony provided a ladder and Deputy Lowe climbed up to retrieve it.

"It's Natalie's, I know it is, she had that peace sign sticker on it." Eric said. "It has a code protected password on it", the deputy announced.

"Let me call her brother Nate to see if he knows it." Reggie said. Nate came to the store immediately after Reggie called him.

"Yes, that is hers and I know the passcode, it's our birth date. 2/5/2000" Nate said. The phone unlocked, it opened to the camera. He handed it over to Reggie.

"Oh my gosh, it's a photo of the front of a white Ford truck. Natalie may have taken this because she knew something was about to happen to her. Maybe, she threw her phone up on the roof or her attacker threw it." She called Ed and asked him to come to the store to retrieve the phone. She also asked the deputies to comb the area for any other evidence.

Reggie received a text.

It read: *Just got my rental car, at the airport, on my way to Birch Creek.* Thank goodness TJ was on his way.

Reggie responded : *Three girls missing, found 1 cell phone, white ford truck is suspect, Freddie lied.* She knew she would fill him in with all the details.

I will head straight to your office, TJ replied.

Reggie drove back to her office. She explained everything she knew so far to Sheriff Johnson. "Bring Freddie in for questioning," the sheriff said.

"Yes, I will."

She walked into her office, grabbed her bag of gummies, in place of a cigarette and dialed Freddie's number.

"Freddie, you know I have been looking for you and I need to talk with you today." "I'm at work right now," he said.

"Either I can come to your work or you can come to my office, your choice," "Can I come when I get off work at 3pm?"

"Yes, be here no later than 4 or I will come looking for you",

Reggie drove back to the wetlands to see if anything changed, she knew she would get a call if it had but she wanted to find a white ford truck in the area. She called Ed to tell him where she was and that she could stop at the GE appliance plant to talk with the head ofsecurity.

She pulled up by the guard house at the GE entrance. She showed her badge and introduced herself.

"I don't have an appointment but I really need to talk with the head of security." She said, "I'm Jack, I am the head of security. How can I help you?'"

"We are conducting an investigation and I know your entrance camera video was very helpful to us. Ed has shared some of the video with me and Sheriff Johnson. I wanted to know if you see a white Ford truck coming and going often along this highway?" She asked. "I know that is a very common truck to be asking about but I thought it might be helpful if you knew of it?" She asked.

"I know most of the cars and trucks that live in this area, at least the ones that pass by here a couple of times a day. A white Ford truck isn't one of them. Of course, with your search and rescue teams out this way, I have seen all types of vehicles coming and going lately." He replied.

"I know it's kind of like a needle in a haystack. We are trying to identify a truck that may be linked to the missing girls."

"I will keep my eyes open for the truck. Let me know if there's anything else we can do to help you out", he stated.

"You already have helped out, thank you." Reggie said as she got back in her jeep. She then drove to the wetland site.

The rescue team was still searching, the water level has gone even further down which is very helpful. She looked at her phone to see the time, she knew she needed to head back to her office.

She walked in her office, threw her cowboy hat on the desk and there sat TJ. She jumped. "Oh, you scared the hell out of me, I wasn't expecting you yet."

"Nice to see you, I got here about 5 minutes ago."

"We have lots to discuss and I got clearance for you to co-investigate with me. You have to stick to the facts, no sensationalism, per Sheriff Johnson." Reggie smiled.

"Yes, ma'am, just the facts, ma'am." He laughed because he knew that sounded cheesy.

"I have Freddie coming in here for questioning again this afternoon. You can watch and listen but can't be in the room with me. He has lied about seeing Kendra the night of the fireworks.

She was seen with him. No one seems to know about some other guy or new boyfriend or a group of people she was with."

"Didn't you say he wasn't trustworthy?' He asked.

"Yes," she rolled her eyes knowing she probably won't get the truth this time either from Freddie.

Freddie arrived right at 4PM. Reggie escorted him to the interview and explained his interview is being recorded.

"What is it now?" he asked. He rolled his eyes and Reggie noticed he was sweating. "Freddie, I need the truth about the night of the fireworks. I have talked to others and it seems as though you have lied to me. Did you talk to Kendra that night?" she asked. "I already told you that I didn't talk to her, she was with some tatted up dude."

"That isn't true, Freddie, and she wasn't intoxicated either according to the people I talked to. Why would you lie about this?" she asked again.

"I don't know who you talked to but they are the liars." Reggie leaned in from across the table.

"I'm just gonna lay it out to you Freddie, you are the number one suspect right now for the disappearance of Kendra and Myra. I need you to talk. I need you to talk and tell the truth."

"Why would I be the number one suspect? You ain't got shit on me, Detective Memphis!" He began to shout.

"Here is what I got on you. You lied about talking to Kendra, you lied about her being intoxicated, you lied about who she was with and you just happened to be at Millstone Pizza the night Myra disappeared. Kendra was with YOU at the fireworks according to others." She pointed her finger at him and moved in closer.

"Also, we now have a 3rd girl missing. Do you happen to know what happened to Natalie?" "That don't mean shit, I was high as a kite the night of the fireworks, as a matter of fact I was higher than the fireworks!" He started laughing. "Are you high now?" She asked.

He didn't answer.

"Who is Natalie? I don't know anyone named Natalie." He said.

"Freddie, you are going to get arrested if you can't tell me the truth." she said.

"Lying ain't no crime! I'm outta here, next time you need information from me, you will have to talk to my lawyer. " He bolted out of the room down the hall out the front door.

Reggie knew she couldn't stop him, she didn't have anything to charge him with at this point. TJ walked in.

"Do you think he actually has a lawyer?" TJ asked.

"His brothers might pay for one for him once again, they have before", she said.

"I need to get checked in to the hotel before all the rooms are gone, It would be nice if Birch Creek had a hotel," he said as he picked up his laptop.

"Stay with me," Reggie blurted out loud before even thinking about it.

"I can't impose on you like that, your boyfriend might not like it." he said.

"Boyfriend? Who has time for a boyfriend? Surely you are not talking to me." She laughed. "No one else is in this room. You are telling me there isn't anyone?" TJ asked.

She rolled her eyes.

"I need to go check-in, talk later?" He asked. "Sure" I offered for him to stay with me, why did I say that? She thought to herself.

She had to debrief with Sheriff Johnson and Ed before going home in order to be ready for the press conference being held in the morning. Ed was busy reviewing all the video footage to see if he could find the Ford truck.

As Reggie drove home, she wondered why Freddie was lying. Now, it was convenient for him to say he was high so he doesn't remember anything. We have to find that Ford truck, we will have to start looking at all the white ford truck owners in the area.

CHAPTER 9

Freddie was feeling the pressure now. He was shaking. He was high and it was the only way he could deal with all of this. He wanted out, he would tell Rum to take back the truck and he wanted out. He dialed his number, no answer. Freddie wondered if he even had this same cell phone number. He knew he changed phones and numbers all the time. He wondered if he was still in this country or had flown somewhere else by now. He tried to call his friends, Woody and Domino, no answer. He knew Woody was in Savannah but not sure where Domino would be after kidnapping Myra and now possibly Natalie. He knew once Rum found out he had refused to do his job, he might send someone after him or just have him killed. Could he tell Detective Memphis he was forced to do what he did? She probably wouldn't believe him if he did confess. Freddie heard all about the search and knew it had to be Domino who threw the cell phones out in the woods. This has gone way too far and I can't go down for all of this. I have to get out of it.

"Fuck them and fuck my brothers."

He wasn't going to help his brothers anymore either. They could find some other way to transport their cocaine in those logs.

CHAPTER 10

TJ drove towards the city limits. He wondered if Reggie really was sincere about him staying at her house. It would certainly be more convenient. Should he stay with her? Why not? He turned around and headed to her house. He was hoping she really meant it and he wasn't making a mistake.

He couldn't help that he was attracted to her, who wouldn't be. He wanted to explain to her what he was dealing with back home in Chicago. She may not want to hear it nor care for that matter.

Reggie pulled into her driveway, there was TJ standing beside his rental car. She smiled at the site of him.

"Did you really mean that I could stay here?" He asked.

"You might as well, we will be working long hours together so you don't need to be driving back and forth out of town. But, of course I will have to ask Sammy if he approves of you staying." she said as she looked back and smiled.

"Well, I might as well turn around and head back to the car, then," he said.

Reggie laughed.

"Follow me." She showed him to her guest bedroom.

"It has a very comfortable bed but I haven't really furnished it yet with other furniture. It's kind of sparse but it does have a large bathroom which makes up for the lack of decor."

"This will be perfect, I appreciate you doing this for me."

"I appreciate you helping me with this investigation. Oh, by the way, the sheriff is doing a press conference in the morning and I think he may need some pointers from you on what to say to generate people to come forward. "

"I can certainly help with that, I'm going to get my things out of the car if you are really ok with me staying here?" He asked one moretime.

"Go get your stuff, I will pour you a drink."

Reggie made her way into the kitchen while he was outside getting his bags. She poured Sammy his cat food as he waited patiently as usual. She realized she hadn't eaten since the pie that morning. She sat down on her sofa, it was still too hot to sit on the back porch. She had not had an overnight guest in a long time, she hadn't planned to have to feed someone else, she decided to order some pizza, everyone loves pizza. TJ walked in wearing a t-shirt and sweatpants.

"I love this bourbon, "he said as he picked up the glass and slowly sipped it. "I'm starving", Reggie said.

"Pizza from Millstone ok with you?" she asked.

"Sounds perfect, I love any kind you want to order. Let me pay for it,"

After the pizza was ordered Reggie began telling TJ everything that has happened in the last few days since he left. As she was telling him what had happened, she realized she was shaking. She had not had this kind of pressure or a case like this since she became a detective. She hesitated a few times while she was talking, realizing the magnitude as she said it all out loud. This was a series of missing girls and somehow it was all connected. TJ listened intently.

"Wow, how are you holding up with all of this pressure?"

"It's my job. I can handle pressure, I just want to find those girls and make someone pay for what they have done. That son of a bitch, Freddie, has something to do with all of this." "Reggie, I'm going to help you. We can solve this."

The doorbell rang.

"It's the pizza, I'll get it," TJ offered.

When Reggie brought plates and napkins into the living room, she noticed TJ was looking at his phone. She wondered if his wife was texting him.

"What will your wife say about you staying with Detective Memphis?" Reggie asked as she raised her eyebrow.

"She won't know." He said not looking up at her.

What the hell kind of response was that? She was thinking to herself. She sipped her drink and looked over at him wondering if he does this kind of thing often. She could feel the heat rising in her neck and face. Who does he think he is? Now she wasn't hungry, she was pissed off.

"She won't know? Do you lie to your wife?" She got up and walked out to the back porch.

TJ wasn't sure what just happened but it was obvious Reggie was mad. He realized he needed to tell her what happened when he went home to Chicago.

"She won't know because I won't be talking to her, she left me." He said as he walked out to sit with her. He looked up at her taking a sip of his bourbon. Reggie put her hand up to her mouth. She felt embarrassed for jumping to conclusions. "What? Oh no, I'm so sorry, I didn't mean to pry." she said.

He was quiet.

"More bourbon?" She asked.

He held his glass up to hand to her. She took the gesture as a "yes." "Let's go back inside and eat our pizza."

She poured more bourbon when she entered the kitchen. TJ went back into the living room. When she came back from the kitchen, Sammy had jumped up in TJ's lap.

"Oh my goodness, I'm sorry, you can make him jump down."

"No, he is fine. He is either fine with me staying or he is plotting how to hurt me.", they both laughed.

"My grandpa used to say that cat's sense when someone is upset or stressed. Supposedly, they sit in your lap to absorb the stress and negative energy to help release it from you. So, I must not be the only one feeling some pressure." She shrugged her shoulders as she said it. "I'm an investigative reporter, so when I had some suspicions about my wife, I investigated. I decided maybe I was not being fair so I hired a private investigator. When I came here last week, my suspicions were confirmed. As soon as I left Chicago, she was with her boyfriend. Actually, the night I was here with you, the PI texted to tell me all the evidence he had on her. I went back to Chicago and confronted her. She admitted it and left."

He took another sip of his bourbon.

"I really am sorry and I don't know what else to say."

"I guess I just brought the mood down this evening." TJ said.

"We both have had a stressful couple of weeks, I'm sorry that I jumped to conclusions earlier, I just had no idea that you and your wife were having trouble."

"It's not trouble, it's called getting divorced. It feels kind of nice to have someone to talk to about it." TJ began telling her that he knew his marriage wasn't going to last after the first 6 months. They drifted apart and he knew she wasn't happy with him. She didn't like that he worked as an investigative reporter, she seemed to think that job was not important. Her new boyfriend was a lawyer with an elite law firm in Chicago.

"Alright, Cowgirl, show me that state champion barrel racing video again!" Reggie laughed and let him watch it again.

"I need to see some college basketball moves - Where are those videos?"

"My mother has plenty that she would be glad to sit down and show you every one of them." TJ rolled his eyes at the thoughts of it and laughed.

They stayed up late talking about past relationships and knowing why they failed.

Reggie lay in her bed awake thinking about the 3 missing girls. She knows the link has to be Frieddie somehow but how? She also thought about how comfortable she feels with TJ. She could easily talk to him.

CHAPTER 11

When she woke up the next morning, she could smell coffee. He is up and making coffee already. She walked into the kitchen but TJ wasn't there. She found him outside looking at her garden.

"You grew all of this?"

"Yes", she replied and started picking tomatoes off the vine. "I'm impressed, a cowgirl and a farmer!," he winked at her.

She was already sweating from the heat from outside, she didn't need any more heat. "I'm going to go take a shower and get ready. I will meet you at my office?"

"I'm going to go eat some cheese grits, you want me to bring you some pie?" he asked. "Of course,"

Reggie stood under the hot water spraying down on her, for a minute or two she just stood there letting it run down her head and body. She needed this time to settle her thoughts and focus on her day. She heard her cell phone ringing. She dried off and quickly searched for where she left her phone. Her phone was on the coffee table in the living room. It was Ed who had called. As she was calling him back, she turned to see TJ slowly and quietly, perhaps sneaking out the back door. Oh my god, had he seen her naked?

"Reggie, hello, are you there?" Ed asked.

"Hey, yes, sorry, I'm here," Reggie hesitated as she was grabbing a towel.

"I viewed the camera from the house near the store. It shows Natalie walking, then she stops and is watching something and then crosses the street. We think this is when she saw the truck and got suspicious. I will show you when you get here."

Reggie got dressed,leaving her hair down wet, she would pull it up after it dried. What made Natalie suspicious? Did she know who was driving the truck? Has she seen it before? What happened to her right before she was going to enter the store? The outside camera was not working at the store, was that planned? Had her attacker planned this and broken the camera a few days before the abduction? All of these thoughts were racing in her mind. She may have known this person from coming into the store. We need to look at all the store's video footage inside and outside from the time Natalie started working there until the day she went missing.

The outside camera footage is probably backed up from before it was broken. That's it, she thought, this attacker had been stalking and planning this for days. When Ed viewed the camera footage before, it was when he was focused on Myra, not Natalie.

Reggie practically ran in the building looking for Ed. He was in the conference room with Sheriff Johnson and TJ. Two pieces of pie sat on the table. As Reggie walked in, she couldn't help but think about TJ seeing her naked, that was why he was sneaking out so she wouldn't know. When she sat down, TJ motioned for her to pick up the pie. She looked up and caught Ed looking at her. Then, he glanced at TJ and gave her a look with both eyebrows raised as if he had a question. "Ed, you want some of this?" she asked as she pointed at her piece. He shook his head no. Sheriff Johnson started asking questions about what facts to include in his press conference and if we had any theories that might generate some talk with the community. We agreed that he should be vague and give an opinion of possibly more than one suspect. Reggie viewed the video that Ed told her about when they talked earlier. She made the suggestion to view all the video footage from the store with a focus this time on Natalie.

"Great idea", Ed said with TJ nodding his head in agreement.

TJ wrote down some talking points for the sheriff to review for his press conference.

The press conference lasted for 5 minutes with only a couple of questions asked. TJ was the one who asked the questions.

"Sheriff Johnson, Can we all assume the missing females cases are all related? And do you have any suspects at this time?

Sheriff Johnson answered yes to both questions and held up a photo of the White Ford truck and asked for anyone with information to come forward. He elaborated to say we have more than one possible suspect. He also disclosed there is a monetary award for information leading to an arrest. He was vague and didn't say how much money nor where the money was coming from. He ended with saying, "no more questions. Another update will be given as needed."

Reggie wasn't sure if there was really a monetary reward or not, she had not heard that mentioned before.

Ed announced it may take a couple of days for him to go through all of the video footage from the Handy Mart.

Shortly after the press conference ended, Sheriff Johnson came back to the conference room.

"Jimmy from City Garage just called. He saw the photo I showed at the press conference. He said the headlights in the photo are not the original factory headlights on that particular truck. Jimmy said he is the one who installed those headlights on that truck. He said the truck belonged to Rumsfeld T. Mason when he worked on it but Rumsfeld died about 5 years ago."

"This is the break we have been looking for," Reggie yelled and held her long slender arms up in the air. "Do we know where Rumsfeld lived? Does he have a living spouse or family that can tell us about the truck?"

"He lived up on the mountain north of the train port. We are looking up the address now. I know he has some family." Sheriff Johnson replied.

"Hallelujah!" Reggie yelled at least 3 times.

"TJ and I can head up that way now." she said. She got the address, grabbed her cowboy hat and headed out the door to her jeep with TJ following her.

"You have a gun with you?", TJ asked.

"Yes, of course, always" Reggie looked at him surprised he asked that question. "I will protect you," she smiled at him.

They drove North out of town up by the train port. There was Captain Joe up on his silo looking through his binoculars down at the port "on watch." He was sitting in his chair with a big umbrella keeping him in the shade.

"The port authority really should pay him for what he does." Reggie said as they passed by waving at him. They turned at the Rock church and headed up the mountain. As the pavement ended the dirt road was leaving a trail of dirty dust behind them, TJ looked over at Reggie, "I doubt there are any black people up here in this territory, makes me a little uneasy", he said. Reggie understood why he was feeling uneasy.

"Everything will be just fine." They drove what felt like 10 miles up the winding dirt road with woods on both sides of the road. Reggie pointed out the driveway that leads to Ms. Doris Bailey's place.

"I still need to take you to meet her. There isn't any water running off the side of the mountain this time of year, too hot and dry. It's actually forest fire weather." Reggie explained. They drove up to a row of mailboxes lined up side by side next to a washed out dirtroad.

"I don't think this is it yet, the numbers on the mailboxes are in the double digits. We are looking for 110." They kept on going straight up the curvy road and their ears were popping. TJ was quiet, seemed to be taking it all in.

"Here's 108, the next one should be 110. It's hard to believe they get mail delivered up here." All of a sudden they saw a big electric gate with stone columns and a matching stone wall surrounding the entrance. The entrance was beautiful with large Norway Spruce trees intertwined with blooming mountain laurel tucked in between the trees.

"Wow!" TJ said.

Reggie pulled up to the gate, no code box or intercom to call anyone. She looked up for cameras but didn't see any cameras either.

"We can't get through here", she said. They tried to look past the gate but it was a long paved driveway that dipped out of sight down the hill.

"Let me leave my card on both sides of thegate."

She wrote: *"Please call me."* Reggie tucked the cards in an upright position in between the rocks on the big columns. They turned around and started back down the mountain.

"That's weird they don't have some type of intercom or code box, how do they accept deliveries?" TJ asked.

"I doubt they get many deliveries up here. When it snows up here, people are stuck for days. The roads get to be a slushy muddy mess, power goes out, trees fall sometimes covering the road." Reggie explained.

"NO, thank you, not me, I couldn't live up here," TJ said as he was shaking his head no.

They met a truck head on on the narrow winding curve in the road, "Well, it looks like Freddie's new vehicle that his brothers told me about," Reggie said as she stopped in the road. It was a silver Toyota Tacoma, it stopped too. She could see that it was Freddie, he blew the horn and yelled:

"Back up some so I can get past you."

Reggie put her jeep in park and got out. She walked over to Freddie's driver side. TJ stepped out of the jeep and stood at a distance but close enough to hear what was being said.

"Freddie, what are you doing up here?"

"Taking a ride up to see a friend, Detective Memphis." He said with a smart ass tone. "What friend would that be?"

"It's really not any of your business, a friend."

"Would you happen to know who lives at the 110 address with the big gate and entrance?" She asked.

"Nope, can't say that I do."

She knew he wouldn't tell her even if he did know. Reggie walked back to her jeep and pulled over as close to the side as she could to let his truck get by.

As he drove by she said, "that nice new truck is going to be filthy." He didn't look her way as he drove on by.

Fuck, she is everywhere, haunting me. Freddie thought to himself. He was looking in his rearview mirror to see if she had turned around to follow him. He didn't see any sign of her jeep. He stopped at the big gate, used his remote to open it. He drove past the big rock wall entrance down the hill leading to the house. He pulled his truck behind the garage in case Detective Memphis happened to be creeping around. He knew she couldn't trespass but she was sneaky. He entered through the kitchen door and quickly walked to the door leading to the basement. The house was silent, as he walked down the stairs, he couldn't hear anyone talking or movement. His heart was pounding, hands shaking, he didn't see any signs of anyone or anything indicating someone had been there. Where were they? Was he too late to rescue them? Had Rum or Domino taken them somewhere? He couldn't let this keep happening, should he tell Detective Memphis what he knows? He knew they would come after him and kill him, if he told anyone anything. Freddie sat down on the basement floor with tears running down his face. He was in too deep. Rum had him captured like a prisoner doing whatever he needed him to do and his brothers had him too. They were wanting another shipment to leave the port this week. Freddie was going to tell them no more shipments and no more working for Rum. He would face their consequences or run. He could disappear.

As they finally got to the paved part of the road, Reggie called Sheriff Johnson. "Do you know if Rumsfeld Mason was a wealthy man?" she asked.

"Yes, he was wealthy, according to Jimmy, the mechanic. When he called to tell me about the truck, he said Rumsfeld owned several vehicles, some were classic cars. He wasn't from this area but moved here after retiring. He said his grandson lives here."

"I need to find his grandson." Reggie said as she finished explaining what they observed up on the mountain. When they arrived back at the office, TJ told Sheriff Johnson he should plan to have another press conference within the next day or two and show photos of all 3 missing girls, show the truck photo again and say we are narrowing in on some suspects.

"I will get the major news media outlets to pick up the story, but get ready for lots of media crews coming to town." TJ said.

Sheriff Johnson agreed to prepare for another press conference the next morning and wanted to prepare the community for the media coverage and the search and rescue teams. Sheriff Johnson explained the search and rescue teams had not found any cell phones or any items related to this investigation. They would be wrapping up the search at the Wetland site this week if nothing is found by the end of the week.

Reggie was craving a cigarette and had lost track of when she last smoked. She stepped outside on the sidewalk and leaned up against the brick building. She wondered where Freddie was going when he was heading up the mountain, what friend was he going to visit, drug dealer, maybe? She needs to find the Mason family and obviously find that truck. She wondered if that truck was still even owned by the Mason family.

Reggie stepped back in to tell TJ and Ed that she was going to pick up lunch for the 3 of them and would be back in about 30 minutes. Reggie drove to The Naked Dog. It was a local hotdog stand off the main roads near the football stadium with every kind of hotdog you can imagine and all kinds of toppings. As she walked up to the takeout window she could smell the aroma of chili and grilled hotdogs. She ordered 3 foot long dogs with side orders of slaw, chili, onions and cheese. She waited at the picnic table outside while they were being prepared. She looked over and noticed a car parked at the side parking space by the building. She got up to look closer at it. It was Myra's car. That's the car Ed had shown her she was driving in the video. She immediately called Sheriff Johnson.

"Sheriff Johnson, I think I found Myra's car, it's parked here at The Naked Dog. I wonder if it's been here since she disappeared or if someone brought it here."

Sheriff Johnson said he would send over a deputy to do forensics on it. If it's her car, he will notify her parents.

"I will talk with the employees here", Reggie explained. Reggie talked with the employees and the manager. None of them had noticed the car until today. They all gave the same answers that they didn't know whose car it was and it wasn't there until today. She had no reasons not to believe what they were telling her. She would follow up if anything was found that negated what they told her.

Sheriff Johnson came in after he arrived back from lunch. His sweet wife, Betty Ann, always cooks his lunch for him. He goes home to eat like clockwork everyday at the same time.

"I stopped by the garage and talked to Jimmy on my way back in. Jimmy said one of Rumsfeld's grandson's renovated and added on to the house after Rumsfeld died. The grandson lives there when he is back in the United States."

"Back in the states? What does he do for a living and where is he when he isn't home?" Reggie asked. TJ was on his computer looking up Rumsfeld and his family.

"Jimmy said he works for some Asian IT company." Sheriff Johnson replied. TJ looked up from his laptop,

"I bet this is him." He read: *Rum Mason, China Tech, CEO.*

"He owns the tech company. It looks like he does a lot of surfing and extreme sports. He is single and was in the Navy." TJ said.

"And he chooses to live on a dirt road in Birch Creek, does that seem odd to you?"

"Let's message him." TJ said. He started typing a message: *We would like to speak with you, Birch Creek Sheriff's Department.*

"That's all you're gonna say?" Reggie asked.

"Yes, I want it to be vague, no need to give him any idea why we want to speak to him." TJ answered and added, "Trust me."

TJ worked on letting his media contacts know about the press conference tomorrow and the developing story. Sheriff Johnson and Reggie called the 3 girls' families to ask them to come to the Sheriff's office in the morning for the press conference. Nate, Natalie's brother, said their parents were on their way to town too. He would bring them in the morning. Ed continued to view all the camera footage from the store from the day Natalie started working there. As they were getting ready to quit work for the day, Ed yelled,

"Whoa, let me enhance this view, this looks like the Rum guy you showed us, do you think that's him?" He asked.

Reggie, TJ and Sheriff Johnson all looked.

"It's hard to tell when I have never met the man nor seen him in person but it looks a lot like the photo on his profile." Reggie said.

"What's the date on that film footage?" TJ asked.

"It's 3 days before Natalie went missing last week." Ed explained.

"Just because he may have been in the Handy Mart, doesn't mean anything, we all go to the Handy Mart, everybody in town goes to the handy mart." Sheriff Johnson explained.

"When he responds back, we can ask him if he has been home lately and has he been to the Handy Mart. I'm still trusting you TJ that he will respond." Reggie smiled.

"He will, you have to remember the time difference if he is in China or wherever he is."

Reggie and TJ left separately to drive back to Reggie's house. Reggie was glad he was in his car, because she wanted to smoke. She was also going to stop to buy a bottle of wine.

When she got home, TJ was waiting on her in the garden because the doors were locked. "I guess I should give you a key,"

He leaned down and was picking some peppers. "This is so cool, growing your own food."

"I will stir fry some vegetables for us tonight, and pour us some wine, if that's ok with you?" she asked.

"Sounds good,"

As Reggie walked into her kitchen, she couldn't remember if he said he was a wine drinker or not but this wine will taste so good paired with the fresh vegetables. Sammy greeted her by rubbing up against her legs. She knew he was ready for his dinner too. TJ had disappeared into the guest bedroom for what seemed like an hour. Reggie had already drunk one glass of wine and poured her second when he walked in the kitchen. She could tell that he had just showered, he smelled so good and was wearing a t-shirt and shorts. She was glad he felt comfortable at her house. She poured his wine. He sipped slowly and said it tasted good. Reggie started chopping up the vegetables for the stir fry. She had already cooked some rice to mix with the vegetables. She set the table while waiting on him too.

"Wine, good food, a beautiful table setting and a beautiful lady to dine with me, what else could I ask for?" TJ said as he pulled out her chair for her.

"Wine makes you a charmer too, not just bourbon." She could feel her face getting warm from the wine. She knew her cheeks would be pink. TJ grabbed the bottle of wine, to top off her glass and his. He raised his glass and said,

"Here's to a great meal and thank you for letting me stay here with you."

"Cheers," she said. When they finished eating, he told her to go sit and he would clean up the kitchen. Reggie didn't try to argue or persuade him not to, she loved the idea of letting him clean up.

As she waited on him to join her, she turned on her TV which she hardly ever watches. She thought maybe they could watch a movie and finish off the wine.

When he came into the living room, she noticed how polished he seemed. HIs t-shirt and shorts looked freshly ironed. She still had on her wrinkled clothes from the day and probably smelled like smoke.

"I'm going to go take a quick shower, Find a movie for us to watch, if you want to." she yelled back as she was walking to her bedroom. She wanted to smell good and be polished and fresh looking too. She showered quickly and decided to put on a t-shirt and shorts too, although she wasn't going to iron hers.

He had picked out a movie to watch. She wanted to laugh because it was a "chick flick" movie. Not the type of movie she likes to watch. She was surprised he had picked it but didn't want to say anything. As she watched the movie about a young, beautiful, single executive woman going back to her hometown for the holidays, Reggie could feel him staring at her. Her cheeks flushed and she turned towards him.

"You're beautiful," TJ said. She wanted to lean over and kiss him, but she restrained herself.

"There's that charm again", she said. "I mean it, Regina Memphis." He said.

"Thank you, that is really sweet," she said.

Now she felt awkward, not knowing what to say. She certainly wasn't interested in the movie, she had already predicted the ending.

"You know what, I can tell you how this movie will end," she said. "I bet we both can predict it. They all end the same."

They moved out to the back porch. The heat had cooled down enough to be pleasant. They sat out on the porch for a while talking before saying goodnight.

She laid in her bed thinking about how he was staring and what he said. Was he drunk?

Did he really mean it? Did he want to kiss me too? She couldn't get comfortable and was tossing and turning so she sat up and turned her light on. Her mouth was so dry, she needed some water. Drinking wine does that to her and next will come the headache. She walked into the kitchen to get a cold glass of water. TJ was standing out on the screened in porch in the dark.

"Hey, are you ok?" She asked.

"I came out here to get some fresh air". TJ said as he was staring out at the garden. She watched him as he rubbed his hands over his face and turned towards her.

"Reggie, you are beautiful and smart, I am attracted," Reggie walked over, interrupting him, not letting him finish his sentence.

"I'm attracted to you too. You are very vulnerable right now after your wife leaving, so I will not take advantage of the situation. I'm going to bed and I will see you in the morning". She said as she walked back inside.

TJ stood there smiling watching her walk back in the house. I sure like this country cowgirl, he thought. She is not like anyone I have ever known. He fantasized about going into her bedroom and crawling into bed with her. He knew he better not, he was a gentleman. He was wondering if she knew he saw her naked. He was sure she saw him sneaking out. He didn't mean to walk in and see, he had left his wallet and came back in to get it.

CHAPTER 12

When Reggie arrived at her office, she couldn't believe what she was seeing. TJ was gone when she woke up and must have anticipated this crowd. The parking lot was filled with News media trucks with lights and cameras already set up. Some of the reporters were already reporting on this breaking story, while spectators were gathering around the podium. Sheriff Johnson had the families of the girls already inside the conference room when Reggie walked in. TJ was there preparing the families to give a statement and also letting them know what would be reported. Reggie could see the look of desperation and sadness on their faces. Reggie was anxious and excited at the same time. She wanted this coverage to help them find those girls and find them alive.

The press conference went as expected with the families pleading for anyone to come forward with information. Myra's mother was crying holding up her daughter's latest school photo. Natalie's parents stood silent while Nate held up Natalie's photo and talked about where she worked and how she just moved to the community and was so happy to be here. Kendra's mother and aunt Doris both pleaded for anyone who saw Kendra the night of the fireworks to come forward. They held up a poster size photo of Kendra. Sheriff Johnson showed the photo of the truck again and said they were narrowing in on the suspects. He reported that Myra's car had been found and they had some evidence that someone else had driven her car. Fingerprints had been taken. No matches had turned up yet in the database.

Several reporters asked questions about when and where each girl was last seen and what we were doing to find them. Sheriff Johnson gave great details of what was known about each girl when they disappeared and detailed what had been done so far. The search and rescue crews were there too standing behind the sheriff.

The parking lot cleared out quickly after the press conference ended with a handful of the news media staying there. TJ explained the process of what the media will do next. Some will go around town asking for comments from the community and some will go to the wetland site and some will stay parked right in the parking lot wanting to be the first to hear any breaking news.

"We have a message from Rum," TJ was looking at his laptop and began to read it outloud: *I just got your message, what is this about? I'm in Buenos Aires and have limited cell service. Here is my phone number so you can try to contact me.*

"Let's call it right now." Reggie said.

Ed agreed and looked up the time difference. "They are only 1 hour ahead of us there."

TJ called the number given. "Hello, is this Rum Mason?"

"Yes, it is."

TJ had his speaker on so they could all hear it. They could hear wind blowing which seemed louder than Rum's voice.

"We need to ask you about your grandfather's White Ford truck. Who owns it now?" TJ asked.

"I own it along with several other vehicles that he collected over the years. Why did something happen to it, was it stolen?" Rum asked.

"We aren't sure if it was stolen or not but it is part of evidence of a criminal investigation.

When were you last here in Birch Creek?" TJ asked. Rum was yelling over the wind sound.

"I was there last week for a couple of days. The truck was in the garage while I was home, I never drove it." Rum yelled.

"Is there a way to prove the truck was in the garage while you were home?" TJ asked. "I got video cameras all around the house, if that helps." Rum said.

"Yes, that could help us. When will you be back home?"

"I have no idea. I wasn't planning to come back anytime soon." He said.

"Do you know Natalie who worked at the Handy Mart?" TJ asked, raising his voice so Rum could hear over the noise.

"I don't know anybody who works at the handy mart. I went in there to buy some beer last week but I don't know anybody there."

Ed nodded his head indicating that was accurate from the video footage. "Alright, we may need to call back with some more questions."

The phone disconnected.

Reggie wasn't satisfied with his responses.

"I need to ask him more questions. Please call him back." TJ dialed his number.

"He's not answering," TJ said.

Reggie composed an email to him: *This is Detective Memphis. I have more questions for you. I need you to call back ASAP. Right now, you are a suspect in a missing person's case. If we don't hear back from you, You will be found by the FBI and brought back here for questioning.*

"Damn, Regina. That's direct." TJ laughed. Ed stuck his hand in the air giving her a high five.

"That's my Reggie," Ed yelled.

Reggie had not had any one on one conversations with TJ yet today. She wondered if he regretted what he said last night. She knew she was attracted to him but knew the timing was all wrong.

"Lunch is on me today," TJ stood up and motioned for Reggie and Ed to come with him.

They dined at the Country Kitchen. TJ sat next to Reggie in the booth. Darlene came over to take their order, she was smiling and looking at Reggie with raised eyebrows again. They each ordered the special of the day which was Fried chicken, rice andgreen beans. Reggie was hungry and knew how good the fried chicken would taste. When Darlene served their meals, Reggie questioned Darlene if she knew any of the Mason family, or Rum Mason?

"No, I don't." Darlene answered. She walked back to the kitchen and brought out 3 pieces of chocolate pie to their table.

"These are on the house, you guys have been working hard on this investigation. I can box them up if you can't eat them right now. I will bring you 3 boxes just in case."

"What a sweet Lady," TJ grinned. "I love this small town."

Reggie's cell phone rang as they were on their way back to the office. It was the dispatcher, "I have a call for you Detective Memphis, It's a nurse from Savannah, Georgia."

"OK," Reggie said with some hesitation.

"Hi, This is John Parker, I just saw the photo of one of the missing women from your town on TV and one of those girls is here in the hospital. I'm a nurse in the ICU here at Savannah Regional. The girl, Kendra, is here in the ICU. She is in a coma. I really can't tell you any more medical information about her because I could get in trouble but I know it's her." He nervously said with his voice shaking.

"How do you know it's her?"

"I saw that big poster of her and on her arm is a tattoo of a flower with a "K" in the middle of it.

This person has the same tattoo and same hair as the girl I saw on the news." His voice was calming down now.

"That is incredible news if it is her. I need your contact information, the hospital information to verify that you are who you say you are and this is a legitimate call. I hope you understand that we have to verify this" Reggie explained.

"Of course," He gave all the information requested.

"Kendra may be in the hospital in Savannah, that was a nurse who said he saw her photo on TV and he seems very sure that the girl in a coma is her.
"

Reggie couldn't believe the words that were actually coming out of her mouth.

"TJ, thank you for getting all of the news media here to cover this story. I'm going to Savannah once we clear all this information." Reggie reached over to hug TJ while he was driving but quickly leaned back, Ed was watching.

Not long after they got back to the Sheriff's office, Ed had confirmed the information.

"All the information reported by John Parker, the ICU nurse checked out." Ed announced.

Reggie grabbed her credentials from her desk drawer and said she was leaving for Savannah. She notified Kendra's mother and Aunt Doris but she didn't want them to make the trip until Reggie could make sure it was her. Reggie promised to call as soon as she identified her.

Sheriff Johnson insisted Reggie drive one of the patrol cars since it was official business. As she was walking out to the car, TJ yelled for her to wait a minute.

"I can go with you," TJ said.

"I would like that. We need to go by my house to get some clothes, Savannah is a long drive and we may need to stay a night or 2. Let me ask Ed to check on Sammy for me." She said as she was walking back towards the office.

It was going to be a long drive with just the two of them. She would try to have some willpower and not smoke. She has already cut the amount way down, she can do this. She packed her suitcase, gave Sammy his food and a belly rub before yelling out to TJ.

"Are you ready?"

TJ was already outside putting his suitcase in the car. Again, TJ looked so polished and groomed and smelled amazing. He grinned as he handed her a bag of gummy bears.

"These are for the trip." "Charmer," she smiled back.

After about 10 minutes into the drive, TJ spoke up.

"I meant what I said last night. You are beautiful and I'm attracted to you Regina. It wasn't the wine speaking and my marriage was over after the first 6 months. I knew it and my wife did too."

Reggie felt awkward again. She stared at the straight long highway in front of her with woods on each side, nothing to really distract her from this conversation.

"I meant what I said too." She could feel him staring at her again which made her very self conscious. She didn't want to let it show but knew her cheeks were flushed again.

"Tell me more about you, Terrence Jenkins," she said changing the subject.

"Well, I was born and raised in Chicago and always wanted to be an investigative reporter. I like to ask questions and interview people. I've worked at the Chicago news for 5 years now, got married after dating 6 months, now getting divorced after 2 years. Now, I'm headed to Savannah with you."

"I think you left lots of information out but it's ok because I like to ask questions too. Do you have any siblings? "

"I have two sisters younger than me who adore their big brother," he responded.

"Hmmm, so, what do they think about your wife.? Is that too personal, you can tell me to shut up if it is." Reggie said not wanting to look over at him.

He laughed.

"You can ask anything you want. Two younger sisters who adore their big brother, what do you think they think of my soon to be ex-wife?" He turned the question back to her.

"My guess is, she was never good enough and they want to say 'I told you so' but won't because they are better than that. Am I close to correct?"

"On the money," TJ wasn't surprised that she knew exactly how they felt.

Reggie kept asking random questions to pass the time while traveling. "What would you do if you were given $10 million?

"Oh, well, I haven't really thought about that. I would write books."

"I would live in a condo at the beach and do volunteer work." Reggie was very confident in her response. She had dreamed about it many times.

TJ had not thought about ever receiving $10 million or any amount because he was very privileged growing up. He already has all the money he will ever need. He works as an investigative reporter because he enjoys it. HIs father is a surgeon and his mother runs the Jenkins Family business because his father wanted to do something different. TJ was like his father in that way. His father's family created a huge cereal company years ago in Chicago. He wasn't sure if Reggie knew of the Jenkins brand of cereal but she had probably heard of the oat bran flakes that the company is famous for. He had not shared with her yet about his family history.

CHAPTER 13

Rum read his email from Detective Regina Memphis. That bitch is trying to threaten me, he thought. That country redneck bitch detective from Birch Creek. He threw his phone down on the table.

"No one threatens me like that." he muttered. Rum was seething with anger. He looked around the cafe to see if anyone was watching him. Nick, his boyfriend, wasn't there to calm him down this time. He rubbed his hand along his squared jaw, contemplating on how to respond back to her.

He wrote: *Detective Memphis, I will be happy to answer any questions you may have for me. I do not appreciate your unprofessional demeanor towards me which leads me to say, you can send any questions through my attorney. I will have him contact you. Respectfully, Rum Mason*

She better not mess with me. He clenched his jaw.

He forwarded his attorney the email: *Mr. Sanders, Please handle this matter.*

Rum dialed Domino's cell number. No answer, he left a message:

"What have you idiots done to get implicated in this? I got the bitch detective wanting to question me."

He dialed Woody next. No answer. He realized Woody had not checked in with him since arriving in Savannah.

"What the hell is going on, Woody?" He slammed the phone down on the table.

CHAPTER 14

When Reggie and TJ arrived in Savannah, Reggie sighed. "I love this town."

"I have never been here, What do you love about it?"

"Everything, the river, the mapped out planned city with all the squares and gardens, the food, River street, the history, the architecture, Tybee Island - Do I need to continue?" She asked.

"Yes, please do."

"Pralines, fudge, seafood, the street vendors. I'm finished, I guess." She laughed.

They headed straight to the hospital. She called John, the nurse, when they arrived. He came down to meet them at the front entrance to escort them up to the ICU unit. He knew it was a matter of police business so he had permission to let them come in to identify her and ask more questions. They walked past the ICU waiting room which was full of family members waiting on the next visiting hour to begin. It seemed as though they all turned to look at her and TJ walking in with John through the locked door that requires a pass code to enter. John commented that the pass code changes every shift to keep people from entering without permission.

The ICU unit looked dark when they entered, their eyes had to adjust to the low lights as they walked past a large circular nurses station with monitors and beeping noises and nurses and doctors walking hurriedly in and out.

John led them over to room #3 where she was laying still on the bed. She had monitors hooked up, a ventilator and IV's and some kind of drainage tube coming from somewhere under the blanket. Reggie wasn't really sure what all of it was but it looked extremely serious. TJ stood back at the doorway and let Reggie walk in. The female laying in the bed had bruises on her face and arms. Cuts on her hands and neck and looked so malnourished. Reggie couldn't see any other parts because her body was covered up. The nurse pulled the cover back to show Reggie the tattoo. Even with the bruises and swelling on her face, Reggie knew it was Kendra and the tattoo confirmed it.

She turned to TJ with tears in her eyes.

"It's her, It's Kendra." Reggie put her hand over Kendra's hand and held it for a few minutes.

TJ spoke up and asked,

"John, what happened? Tell us about her medical condition and prognosis?"

"I'm limited in what I can tell you but I can tell you how she got here." John pointed for them to follow him out of her room into a conference room. John explained that it's better to talk away from Kendra because you never know what patients can hear or comprehend.

"She was brought in by a Savannah police officer. Officer Nelson found her down by the river laying on a park bench. He thought she was a homeless person just sleeping but when he couldn't wake her up, he saw all of her injuries. We can tell her family a little more about her care and medical condition. Officer Nelson can probably tell you some more details too.

"I need to call her mother and aunt right away. They will be on their way as soon as we hang up the phone. John, thank God you saw her photo on the news and identified her."

"The big poster is what really helped because I could see that tattoo." John replied. "We will be here in town for a couple of days gathering information and checking on her condition and prognosis."

"I would be glad to write up a letter of appreciation for your service for your superiors if you wish." TJ added.

"Not necessary but thank you." John gave them a paper with instructions on how to call in to the unit, visiting hours, and his supervisor's contact information too in case he was off duty and Officer Nelson's contact information.

"John is truly an angel", Reggie told him as he led them to the elevator.

Reggie practically ran outside to call Doris Bailey. TJ agreed to call the sheriff while she talked to Kendra's mother and Doris.

"Mrs. Bailey, Kendra is here in the hospital. They will tell y'all more when you get here. Her dr. will meet with you. I will text you the address and the nurses contact information."

Reggie could hear Doris crying and relaying all the information to Kendra;s mother who was at Doris's house.

"We will be on our way within an hour."

Reggie then called Officer Nelson, she was told he was off duty until tomorrow morning. "Can I have his personal cell or get a police report? I am Detective Memphis from Birch Creek, it's important that I talk to him."

"I can put you through to his supervisor," The dispatch operator put her on hold and then connected her to a voicemail.

"Well,hell," Reggie said, after she left the Captain a message.

"I'm starving, let's go eat some good "low country boil" food, she told TJ.

"I have never eaten that but I'm willing to try it," TJ was agreeable to any suggestions Reggie made; she liked that.

"I'm going to teach you how to eat crawfish, city boy." She winked at him.

"That was the best food I have ever eaten, I am so full right now," TJ rubbed his belly acting like it was poking out which it wasn't. Reggie was glad to see him enjoying himself. It sounded like he has not had much happiness lately from what he had shared.

"We need to find a hotel to stay in for a couple of nights." Reggie looked over to see his reaction.

"Let's find one near the hospital", he suggested.

Reggie closed the curtains in her hotel room right away upon entering. Her window was right across from the hospital on a busy street. She turned on the TV hoping to block out the noise of the traffic below. She looked around, the room was average and clean. She took her shoes off and laid on the bed staring at the TV. She wasn't listening to it, her mind was wandering. What had Kendra been through in the last few weeks? Who did this to her and why? Will she survive? We will catch whomever is responsible.

Her phone vibrated, it was a text from TJ. *"Can I come visit you?" "Sure."* She was curious as to what he wanted.

TJ walked in holding a styrofoam takeout food box.

"Which piece do you want, strawberry cheesecake or the chocolate silk pie?"

"Chocolate. I thought you were so full and couldn't eat anything else?" Reggie picked up the box, opening it up.

"Well, I wanted to get you some pie and then I couldn't resist once I saw all the desserts." He smiled, taking the plastic forks and napkins out of the plastic wrapper.

"This is so good, I won't be able to eat it all but I can save it for breakfast," Reggie took a couple more bites and then put the rest in the small mini fridge. She turned around and noticed TJ had some cheesecake on his lip.

"You got some of it on the side of your mouth", Reggie pointed to the corner of his mouth. "Where?" he said as he was wiping the other side of his mouth. She moved closer.

"No this side."

"Where, show me," He was smiling that half grin showing that dimple. "Wait, you are teasing me." she said as she moved closer.

He leaned in and kissed her.

Oh, those cheesecake tasting, wonderful lips that she kissed back. He put down his cheesecake on the nightstand in between the 2 queen beds. He moved over next to her and held her face gently and kissed her again. He was giving her the look again, those hungry eyes could devour her.

Reggie stood.

"We can't do this right now, it's not the right time." He looked puzzled.

"Our focus has to be on solving this crime, and I want everything to be right when the time comes." Reggie explained as she kissed his cheek. TJ stood up.

"Ok, when the time comes."

TJ went back to his hotel room. He worked on an article that seemed to be changing each day as this mystery continued. He emailed his broker to let him know that part of the reward money would be going to John Parker, the ICU nurse. He had not told Reggie that he was paying the reward money for any information that helped locate these girls.

An email appeared from Rum. He read Rum's response to Reggie's earlier email. He knew this was going to fuel Reggie's fire.

"Reggie, you got an email back from Rum." TJ texted.

"Can you come back to my room?" She asked.

As he entered her room, she quickly said, "Read it to me." He read it without trying to put any emphasis on any of the words but Reggie caught on to the tone of the email.

"He is such an ass. He now wants me to go through his attorney, sounds like he is hiding something."

"Hand me your laptop please so I can respond."

Mr. Mason, please let your attorney know that you are expected to come in for questioning within the week.

"Here, read it but I already hit send." She smiled. "Damn, direct and to the point, Regina."

CHAPTER 15

The next morning, Reggie received a call from Officer Nelson.

"He can meet us at the hospital," she told TJ as they were walking out of the building. "We can check on Kendra and then he will take us to where he found her and give us some more information.

They entered Kendra's ICU room. Her mother and aunt had gone to get some rest, they had been up there all night.

"They were able to talk with one of the doctors to get a better understanding of her condition, there has been no change in her condition overnight. They will be completing some more tests today."

"Thank you, I'll call her aunt later." Reggie was holding Kendra's hand again, hoping she could feel it.

Officer Nelson came in to check on Kendra as they were walking out. He introduced himself. "I'll just be a minute, then we can go." Reggie could tell he was as anxious as the rest of them just wanting her to be ok.

They drove down to the river on the famous "River Street" with its cobblestone street running along the edge of the Savannah river. Those old buildings had such history to each of them.

Officer Nelson pointed out the ones which were supposedly haunted by the old pirates that used to dock here. They parked and walked over to where he found Kendra.

"When I saw her, I thought she was asleep on her stomach and I was trying to wake her up to get her to move on for the day. Sometimes we have to tell the homeless to move on away from the crowds on the street. She wouldn't budge. I then noticed her arms all cut and bruised so I turned her on her side and noticed how swollen her face was and it was covered in bruises and cuts too. Her neck was cut and looked like a rope burn around it. I scooped her up and called EMS. I could barely feel a pulse. She was dirty and clothes were torn too. She never woke up during the time I was with her. One thing that stood out, she had a band around her wrist with some numbers and initials on it. I took a photo of it. At first, I thought it was from a local bar or nightclub but I have checked in the last several days and none of the local ones have bands like this." He showed Reggie and TJ the photo. It was a rubber looking band with letters and what looked like a serial # on it.

"What could that be for?" Reggie asked. She looked over at TJ who seemed to be looking it up on his phone to see if he could find some type of wrist band.

"I'm not sure yet, still checking it out. The hospital saved her clothes and the wristband so we are analyzing it for DNA. Let's go to my office, we can see if forensics has any information yet."

Reggie called Kendra's Aunt Doris.

"The doctor told us that she had some internal bleeding from being beaten and they have her in a medically induced coma so her body can heal and she won't be in as much pain. They plan to do some more tests today and reduce the medicine to let her wake up. She is going to heal and be ok, Reggie!" Doris began to cry.

"That is wonderful news, I am so happy." Reggie said as they were pulling into the Savannah police station.

The Savannah Police station was a modern looking building with modern art sculptures out in front surrounding a water fountain. It had four floors with a huge marble staircase in the front lobby leading up to the second floor. They took the elevator up to the fourth floor where officer Nelson worked. The forensic analyst came over to greet us and asked us to follow him. We entered a large room with tables lined up in a row. It looked like evidence items were being scanned and analyzed. He led us over to a computer.

"Here is what we have found. This photo is a man named Woody Billings who was in our database already for some assault charges. His DNA was found on Kendra's clothes. He has been arrested in the past for assault here in Savannah and in Florida. His work history shows that he mostly works on ships which keeps him in international waters most of the time.

"Why would Kendra be with him?" Reggie looked at TJ knowing he was probably looking up everything he could find on this guy.

"There is something else I must show you. The analyst showed them another photo of a shipping container. Do you see the serial number and letters on the side of that container, it matches Kendra's wristband."

"Oh my God," Reggie sat down in a nearby chair before her knees buckled under her. "The train port that ships containers from Birch Creek here to Savannah to load on to the ships, oh my God. It's Freddie, I know he has something to do with this. Was Kendra being trafficked by Freddie?"

"That container is owned by a company called "China Tech." the analyst announced.

Reggie jumped up and said, "We have to alert your Police Chief and my sheriff, we have to call in the FBI now."

The pattern of disappearances in Birch Creek was too coordinated, too systematic to be random. This is bigger than she could have imagined. Without wasting a moment, she walked out to call Sheriff Johnson.

"Sheriff Johnson, we need to talk," she said urgently. "We are dealing with something much bigger than missing females from Birch Creek, it's an international human trafficking ring." Sheriff Johnson's voice cracked as he tried to speak. Reggie could hear the gravity of the situation sinking in as she outlined her findings and suspicions.

"We have to involve the FBI right away," Reggie said firmly. "This is beyond our jurisdiction, we are dealing with organized crime here, and we are going to need all the resources we can get. Officer Nelson will alert his sheriff here in Savannah."

"Reggie, you have to be sure of this," Sheriff Johnson said. "I'm texting you some photo evidence right now."

Sheriff Johnson agreed to let her call the nearest FBI field office. Reggie's hands shook as she made the call knowing once the feds got involved, her role in the investigation would inevitably change.

As she hung up the phone, Reggie felt a sense of determination wash over her. She may have alerted the authorities to the scope of the problem, but she wasn't going to sit idly by and let someone else take over. Birch Creek was her hometown, her people, and she was going to see this through to the end. She would gather more evidence, knowing that every piece brought them one step closer to uncovering the truth behind not only the Birch Creek disappearances but the sinister operation lurking beneath the surface of their quaint little town.

As the FBI convoy approached the shipping port in Savannah, the sun was just beginning to rise, casting a bright hue over the sprawling industrial complex. Towering cranes loomed overhead, their shadows stretching across the maze of shipping containers stacked high like giant Lego blocks. Reggie spotted Agent Miller, the lead agent she talked to the day before. She recognized him from the credential photo she had seen when looking up the field office. HIs expression looked grim and focused. Surrounding him was a team of agents, all armed and ready for whatever awaited them at the port. Reggie knew it could develop into a dangerous situation quickly. As Reggie approached agent Miller, TJ and Detective Nelson and the Savannah Sheriff accompanied her to introduce themselves and welcome the FBI agents. She could see the agents already scanning the area, alert for any signs of suspicious activity. The atmosphere was tense with the shipping port workers looking at all the cars arriving. Their trust was scarce and secrets ran deep among each team of workers. There seemed to be a noticeable silence among the dock workers but the agents seemed undeterred as they approached a group of workers flashing their badges. The majority of the workers didn't speak English and those who did gave evasive responses to the questions. The FBI team split up to search and attempt to interview the port officials. Reggie and the others were quickly alerted by the FBI announcing they were locking down the port to search all the containers, especially those which had come in from Birch Creek port and any others owned by China Tech. This lockdown would delay ships coming and going for a couple of days.

After checking on Kendra at the hospital, Reggie and TJ headed back to Birch Creek to continue the investigation of Myra and Natalie's disappearance, knowing they were all somehow connected but the FBI only had jurisdiction currently on Kendra's case.   Doris Bailey told Reggie she would call her as soon as Kendra was talking and able to tell what happened. As they drove back to Birch Creek, Reggie's thoughts were swirling with doubt and frustration. She had given her best but was it good enough? She knew the FBI had to take over but she was feeling sidelined and inadequate. Feeling the weight of this case pressing down on her, she looked over at TJ and began pouring her heart out to TJ confessing her fears and insecurities.

"I just feel like I'm not good enough." She admitted, her voice trembling with emotion. "I thought I could handle all of this, but now I'm not so sure."

There were a few seconds of silence as TJ gathered his thoughts. He began to speak with a soft and reassuring voice.

"Reggie, listen to me, you are a strong woman and one of the most determined people I know. You have dedicated your life to your career and it is normal to be feeling like you're inadequate in a case such as this. Do not dismiss all you have already done in this case and how it has led to something huge."

During that moment, Reggie realized how lucky she was to have met TJ and have him as her confidant. She knew he was sincere and truly believed in her. She took a deep breath and after letting his words sink in, she had a new found determination to find these girls and seek justice.

<h1 style="text-align:center">CHAPTER 16</h1>

A press conference had been held before they returned to Birch Creek to explain the FBI was taking over part of the investigation. Sheriff Johnson briefed her and TJ about it.

"Oh, Reggie, you got a letter here from some law firm," he said as he handed her the envelope. She looked over at TJ.

"Well that was quick-Rum's attorney I presume." She opened the letter and read it outloud:

"Dear Detective Regina Memphis,

I am writing to you on behalf of my client, Mr. Rum Mason, CEO of China Tech, in response to your recent attempts to contact my client directly regarding your ongoing investigation.

Firstly, I must express my concern over the manner in which you have chosen to conduct yourself in this matter. Your actions are potentially disruptive to my client's daily operations and personal affairs. Furthermore, I must remind you that Mr. Mason is a busy individual with numerous professional obligations. While he remains committed to cooperating with law enforcement to the fullest extent possible, he cannot be expected to drop everything at a moment's notice to accommodate your requests. Any communications regarding this matter should be directed through my office, and we will respond in a timely manner.

In light of the above, I must inform you that Mr. Mason will not be complying with your request to appear for questioning within a week. Any further attempts to contact him directly will be considered harassment and will be dealt with accordingly......"

"Blah, blah, blah - I can't read anymore." Reggie rolled her eyes.

"Reggie, do not get caught up in a power struggle with Rum Mason. We will deal with him when necessary." Sheriff Johnson motioned for her to hand him the letter.

TJ was working on the latest news update for his Chicago station to air that evening. Reggie left him at the office while she drove up to the train port. The first thing that Reggie saw was Captain Joe up on the silo. What the hell; I should talk to him. Reggie parked her jeep and climbed up the steps.

"Wow, what a view from up here, you can see farther than what I thought." Reggie said to Captain Joe.

"Oh yes, I see all kinds of beautiful sunsets and sunrises and sometimes strange things going on around here." Captain Joe smiled. He was dressed in a Hawaiian shirt and shorts wearing a baseball cap.

"Strange things, like what?"

"I keep a list right here when I see something strange." Captain Joe pointed to a notebook on his table. Reggie opened it up. He had written a list which covered several pages in the notebook. The list showed the date and time and what he had seen.. She read examples of the list - *June 28, 7 ducks landed on a train car, June 22, fire trucks appeared at the port with sirens on but no fire, May 9th, A tour bus came to the port asking for a tour but they were turned away. The newest entries were from several dates in July - unidentified flying objects flew over the port for several minutes then disappeared.* This had been entered several times this month. Reggie questioned Captain Joe.

"You have been seeing a UFO flying over the port?"

"Yes, it is black with legs that look like a spider. It flies around for a few minutes and then flies away. I usually see it at night. The train seems to stop for a few minutes after it flies away."

"That's very interesting, can you call me next time you see it?" Joe shook his head agreeing to call her.

When she left Captain Joe, she stopped at the entrance guard house to talk with Michael. "I am here to see you this time Michael," she smiled.

"Oh, I knew you would come around and answer my prayers," he laughed, putting his hand over his heart.

"Freddie isn't working today," he said.

"I wanted to ask if you have seen any drones flying over the port? Captain Joe has seen them several times this month. He said it's mostly at night."

"No, I haven't but I leave at 5:00 PM everyday. We don't allow any entrance after 5 PM for trucks to pick up or deliver. I can ask some of the inspectors if they have seen any. The port doesn't ever close but we restrict access after 5 PM." Michael explained.

"Thank you, very helpful, call me after you talk with the inspectors." Reggie smiled and pulled away. She couldn't resist the urge–she grabbed a cigarette. Reggie drove past Freddie's trailer. It looked like he was home, the truck was parked out front. She debated about stopping but knew she needed to have some more information before trying to talk tohim again.

Ed was in the conference room when she arrived back at the Sheriff's office.

"Ed, can you get a schedule of when Freddie has worked this month? Also, would you know why drones would be flying over the port at night? Who has drones around here?" Reggie sat down next to Ed. "Why would drones fly over then disappear and then the train stops for a few minutes after they disappear?"

"Slow down Reggie", Ed waved his hands in the air. TJ had walked in while Reggie was asking all these questions.

"Drones could be checking to see who is there, what's being inspected, what the inspectors are doing, they could be a distraction too for the inspectors." TJ answered. Reggie sat silent for a few minutes.

"When the drones disappear the train stops, possibly for an inspection or to load something on the train, that's it" She shouted.

"Reggie, Mr. Adams was just here. He is upset with how this investigation is being handled. He wants a male detective who he thinks will be more aggressive". Sheriff Johnson uttered. "They heard about Kendra being found and are hoping Myra is next to be found."

"What did you tell him?" Reggie could feel her stomach tightening. TJ and Ed were watching her reaction as the sheriff answered her.

"I told him you were top notch and the best detective in the tri-state area. He wasn't happy and said he is going to the media this afternoon to demand you be taken off this investigation. I'm going to give him some time to cool down, no changes to be made yet."

"Yet?" she thought. She walked outside to get some fresh air and smoke. She remembered Natalie asking her, Is it 1964 in this town?

"Yes, it is Natalie," she said out loud. He wants a male detective who will be more aggressive!

CHAPTER 17

"Detective Memphis? It's me, Freddie." His voice was strained on the other end of the phone.

"What is it Freddie,?" She could tell his call seemed urgent by the tone and strain of his voice.

"I need to talk to you but not over the phone, can you come over to my place?" His voice was shaking with fear. Reggie hesitated for a moment, her instincts screaming at her to proceed with caution. She could tell something was different, the tone of his voice stirred some empathy within her.

"Yes, I can". She confirmed.

"Please come alone?", he asked. As she drove up to his trailer, she knew he had probably gotten word that the FBI knew he was involved.

When Freddie opened the door, she immediately noticed his busted lip, black eye and bandaged up hand. He motioned for her to come inside while he put his dog out the front door. Alone in the small living room, Freddie struggled to find the right words to say. It was obvious he was scared and nervous.

"What happened to you?" Reggie asked.

"That's not important, I need to tell you something. Detective Memphis, I'm not as bad of a person as you think I am."

"Prove me wrong, then Freddie. Tell me about your involvement with these girls disappearing."

Freddie stared down at the floor. The dog was barking outside. As he started to talk, the front door swung open, Reggie jumped up and instinctively grabbed her gun, her heart was pounding in her chest. Had Freddie set her up? Freddie's eyes were fixed on hers as if pleading to her silently to stay calm. She realized it was Phil and Simon as Phil entered.

"Whoa now, it's just us coming to see our little brother," Phil put his hands up in the air. "What are you doing here?" Phil asked.

"Is he in some trouble?" Simon was pacing back and forth outside in front of the door. He stuck his head in.

"We need Freddie to come help us with some work."

Reggie could tell Freddie looked nervous. She knew he had always been intimidated by his brothers. She was so close to Freddie giving her information and now they had interrupted and killed the moment. She knew he wouldn't tell her anything with his brothers around.

"I was just here asking him some more questions. I'm doubting he can offer you much help, looks to me like he needs some rest." Reggie said as she was walking out the door.

"Stay in touch with me, Freddie." As she climbed up into her jeep, she couldn't believe what she was seeing, a black drone in the back of Phil's truck. She quickly took a photo and backed out of the driveway. She called TJ to let him know that Freddie's brothers owned a drone.

"Damn, Regina, you went up there by yourself? You could have been the next victim." His voice was raised with concern.

Around 10PM, that evening, Doris called Reggie with some news. She motioned for TJ to come closer as she turned it on speaker so he could hear the conversation.

"Reggie, Kendra is awake and remembers what happened. She is talking to the FBI right now. She told me information that I wanted you to hear from me. She is remembering bits and pieces as she becomes more coherent."

Doris began telling Reggie what Kendra told her: "Freddie took Kendra the night of the fireworks to the train port to show her how it all works.

They stopped at his trailer first so he could make them some drinks. She said she thought he was trying to impress her by showing her how the cars are loaded and the inspections worked. They opened up a shipping container and went inside. Kendra said she couldn't believe it, it had been fixed up like a room. It had a bed, sofa, and a little refrigerator. She started feeling tipsy and they started kissing on the bed. He handcuffed her to the bed. She passed out after that. She remembers waking up with the train moving, she doesn't know how long she had been asleep. Her mouth was taped, she was handcuffed to the bed. Her feet were tied with a rope. After some time, she knew the train had stopped. Maybe a day or two had passed, she wasn't sure. A man opened the door and unlocked her handcuffs and took the tape off of her mouth. He threatened he would kill her if she tried to scream or run. He held a gun to her head. He gave her some water and a sandwich. She said she kept asking him questions and he would never respond. She wasn't sure if he spoke English or not. She could hear some sort of machine outside but wasn't sure what it was.

The day she escaped, she had managed to get her feet untied before the same man came in to check on her. He uncuffed her to let her eat and took the tape off her mouth. She started kicking him as hard as she could. He was hitting her, trying to choke her with the rope but she kept on fighting. He cut her several times with his knife. She must have been screaming really loud because she heard voices outside yelling, trying to open the container door. Two men came in and were fighting with him. She managed to get out while they were fighting. She crawled down in between the containers and ran to the dock as fast as she could and never looked back. She was bleeding everywhere and then must have passed out on the park bench where the officer found her."

"Thank you Doris, for telling me all of this. I can't imagine what she has been through. Your niece is one tough lady. The man she is describing must be Woody Billings. The FBI is trying to find him. I assume Freddie will be arrested by the FBI very soon", she added.

"I think she will continue to remember more and give more details. If she tells anything else after talking with the FBI, I will call you."

"Thank you so much." Reggie said as she was hanging up the call.

Once again, Reggie laid awake, thinking about what Kendra had been through and wondering if she would be able to find Myra and Natalie. She tiptoed into the guest bedroom and climbed in bed with TJ.

"I can't sleep."

TJ pulled her close and put his arms around her. She felt safe with him, he smelled so good and she wanted his warm body next to her. He ran his fingers gently down her hair, stroking it until she fell asleep.

CHAPTER 18

Reggie sat on her back porch drinking her coffee. Sammy was laying in his usual spot. She was thinking about Myra's father, Mr. Adams. He must have cooled off. There had been no more demands made by him that she was aware of. She knew Sheriff Johnson must have handled it and reassured him they were all working together on this case. Reggie was feeling down because TJ was going back to Chicago today to 'wrap up some loose ends', as he had described it.

TJ appeared in the doorway with the pot of coffee in his hand.

"Need some more?" he gestured and poured it without waiting for her to answer. He sat down beside her and gave her that look again that she has grown to accept without the awkward feeling of it.

"I want to come back here in a few days, do you want me to?" He asked. "Yes, I do." She kissed his lips.

"TJ what if I don't find those girls in time?"

"We, me and you, the FBI and the whole country will find them." He said as he hugged her. She wanted him to keep hugging her.

"Regina, you have already done a great job on this case, if it wasn't for you, we wouldn't be this far into solving it." She liked when he called her Regina.

"I will finish up my story on the plane that will air tonight. It will recap everything so far and plead for the public to come forward. I have to go, I don't want to miss my flight. I will call you". TJ stood and kissed her forehead.

TJ didn't want to leave Reggie right now but he had to go back to Chicago to take care of business dealings, check-in with his boss at the news station and most importantly make sure his attorney had handled all the divorce proceedings. He wanted to put that marriage behind him. He had an overwhelming sense of urgency to share all about his life and family with Reggie but knew it would all come with time. He was drawn to Reggie like no one ever before. He would come back to Birch Creek as soon as he could.

CHAPTER 19

Freddie was losing his mind at this point. He was stoned and sweating as he drove over to Detective Memphis' house. His back and sides were bruised and his kidneys felt swollen. He had been beaten again by his brothers when Reggie left his house. He kept telling them he had not told Detective Memphis anything about the drugs. He had to change this situation. Rum, Woody and Domino were not communicating with him anymore which made him even more scared. He knew they were coming after him too since he refused to help anymore. There is only one way he could get out of this, he knew what had to bedone.

As Reggie was backing out of her driveway, she noticed Freddie's truck was out on the street blocking her driveway. She parked and jumped out of her jeep walking towards the bottom of her driveway. Freddie was standing beside his truck facing her. She immediately noticed Freddie was holding a gun to his head. She grabbed her gun from her holster.

"Freddie, put the gun down." she pleaded.

He was crying,

"No, I have to tell you something and I have to do this."

"Freddie, whatever it is, we can discuss it, I can help you, just put the gun down." She continued to plead.

"NO, I want you to know that I'm not as bad as you think. After Kendra, I wouldn't do it anymore. I told him that I couldn't do it." His hands were shaking so much she was afraid he was going to pull the trigger at any second.

"You told who?" she asked.

He kept muttering as if he didn't hear Reggie.

"The night Myra disappeared, I tried to stop it from happening. He said I had to keep helping or I would be killed. He bought me the truck as payment." He was shaking, still pointing the gun at his head.

"Freddie, calm down, let's talk, tell me who you are talking about." Reggie was holding up her hand trying to motion for him to sit down. She was trying to grab her phone but not wanting to make any sudden movements. She dropped it on the pavement. He pointed the gun at her.

"Don't touch your phone, Detective, leave it on the ground." He yelled.

"Ok, Freddie, I'm leaving it there. Freddie, let's sit and talk all of this out, put the gun down now." she yelled. He turned the gun back on himself.

"I was trying to take care of Myra and Natalie but now I don't know where they are." Freddie said as he was wiping the tears on his face.

"Who said you had to keep helping or you would be killed?" Reggie asked.

"Rum Mason. . I can't take it anymore, I can't do it. He is selling these girls." Freddie closed his eyes, still holding up the gun.

"Freddie, put the gun down, please. You have given some helpful information." Reggie was shaking but her adrenaline was kicking in, she was slowly walking towards him. This is not the way to solve all of this. You can help us, Freddie."

Freddie slowly leaned against his truck sliding down to sit on the pavement. The gun is still pointing at his head.

"Freddie, who beat you up?" Reggie asked as she walked closer to him. "Don't come any closer. My brothers."

She stopped, not taking her eyes off him. He was beginning to calm down and lowered the gun. "It's the only way, I'm sorry, Detective Memphis." He quickly pointed the gun at his temple and closed his eyes.

Reggie yelled "NO" as he was pulling the trigger. A loud shot rang out. He was dead. She ran towards him and dropped to the pavement. It was an image she would never forget.

It seemed as though the whole town showed up at her house within minutes. Sheriff Johnson and Ed ran towards her. She was still sitting in front of Freddie's dead body. Reggie had never seen anyone kill themselves. Her father had threatened it many times while in a drunken state but she always knew he didn't mean it. Her father would get drunk and start feeling sorry for himself. He would say he was a loser and couldn't do anything right, then he would get angry and wave his gun around saying he needed to just kill himself. He would end up crying and then pass out. His gun disappeared one day, she wasn't sure who took it but was thankful it was gone. She assumed her grandfather took it away but never mentioned it.

The media, EMS, sheriff deputies, neighbors and others were out on the street. The FBI were on their way too. Freddie would have been arrested that day. Reggie sat with Sheriff Johnson and Ed on the back porch.

"His brothers beat up Freddie but I don't know why," Ed and the Sheriff listened as she was replaying the event outloud, desperately, looking for answers.

"I know his brothers have something to do with the drones at the port. Were they making Freddie do something for them, like watch the inspectors, or distract them or load something onto the train? Do they work with Rum?"

"We will get to the bottom of this, Reggie." Sheriff Johnson patted her on the shoulder.

TJ had just entered the airport when he saw the news on the overhead screen. It was breaking news and he saw Reggie's house in the background.

"Oh my God." He started running back out of the airport to his car. He couldn't comprehend how quickly all of this had transpired within a short amount of time. When he arrived at Reggie's house, he parked down the street and had to push his way through the crowd of people that had been blocked off from the crime scene. One of the deputies let him through the barricade.

Freddie's body was still in the street covered with a bloody sheet. All the deputies seemed to work in unison, each knowing what they had to do. The FBI was arriving on the scene when he walked up the driveway.

Reggie heard a familiar voice asking if she was ok, it was TJ. She felt relieved to hear him walking in. He ran over and embraced her and kissed her forehead. Reggie noticed Ed was watching their interaction. She didn't care.

"Reggie, I shouldn't have left, I can't believe what happened, are you ok?" "I'm ok, just a little shocked by it all. TJ, I tried to stop him but it didn't work."

They could hear voices in the crowd getting louder and louder and the deputies telling them to stop. It was Simon and Phil trying to push through the crowd. Reggie could hear Freddie's brothers screaming out front.

"Detective Memphis, you caused this," they kept yelling.

"To hell with them. They will be arrested soon." Reggie said as she lit her cigarette.

"TJ, Freddie told me that Rum was getting paid to traffic girls and he said, 'I couldn't do it anymore after Kendra.' He tried to stop it from happening to Myra that night she disappeared. He said he tried to take care of Myra and Natalie but now he doesn't know where they are. He said his brothers beat him up but didn't say why. I think Freddie was headed up to Rum's house that day when we passed him on the road."

Sheriff Johnson came in to tell Reggie that the FBI had a search warrant for Rum's house on the mountain and Freddie's trailer. They would be going up there now. Reggie wanted to go but sheriff Johnson told her she had to stay here to be interviewed by the FBI.

"All of the shipping containers at the Birch Creek port have to be searched. Those girls could be in one. Freddie said he didn't know where they were now, we have got to find them. We also have to bring in Freddie's brothers for questioning. They have something to do with all of this."

After Reggie's interview, the FBI investigator informs her and the sheriff that an informant was able to talk with some of the men who work down on the docks in Savannah. The rumor is that Woody was stabbed to death by the two men that heard Kendra being attacked. The informant was told his body was thrown into the Savannah river. No one is telling who those men were because everyone feels Woody's murder was justified.

The sheriff and others cleared out to leave Reggie at home to "re-group" as Sheriff Johnson had described it.

"What the hell, I don't need to re-group. You missed your flight back to Chicago," Reggie said.

"It's more important to be here with you," He held her hand.

Reggie spoke up after a few minutes of silence.

"I guess the FBI will be taking over all of these cases now, damn!" They better not try to shut me out of this case."

CHAPTER 20

Rum had fled to Italy. He heard the breaking news the FBI had shared. He would be hiding until he could figure out his next move.

"They will never catch me nor charge me with any crimes because I am innocent." he told his lover, Nick. Nick was at least 10 years younger and very impressionable. He would believe anything "The Great Rum" had to say. The white Ford truck was no longer in his possession. Woody Billings had taken care of the truck before he was killed. It was now scrap metal thanks to Woody's team of car thieves. Rum was told it had been taken apart piece by piece. Some parts were destroyed and some sold but no one would be able to identify it anymore.

"Those stupid backwoods detectives should have gotten their hands on the truck once they knew about it but it was too late!" He laughed and poured himself some fine Italian wine. I have enough money to stay hidden for a long time.

Nick felt reassured that Rum knew what he was doing and never commented about his business dealings, mostly trying to ignore what he overheard. It was better that way not to know much about it.

"I know you're innocent, Rum." Nick smiled and kissed his cheek as he walked out the door to do some shopping. Nick loved shopping but knew to keep a low profile when going out. No one really knew he was linked to Rum and not many people there knew of Rum. Nick will buy some necessities and some decor for their lovely Italian apartment. He wasn't sure how long they would be staying there but always wanted their home to be comfortable and decorated in his elegant style. He knew Rum didn't care what he bought or how much he spent. He was always satisfied with Nick's style and purchases made.

CHAPTER 21

Reggie was at home for the rest of the afternoon, sheriff's orders. She was pissed off and felt like this was wasting time. TJ had finished up his story for the evening news. TJ stepped into the hallway when he received a phone call. Reggie could only hear his side of the conversation but wondered what he was talking about.

"I can't come right now, Detective Memphis needs me here right now. We had some new developments in this case today. I know I missed it, I am sorry."

What did he miss and who is he talking to? she wondered.

"Yes, I will be there, I won't miss the dedication, I promise. I love you too, I will, yes, ok, bye." he said as he hung up his phone.

What was he talking about, a dedication, what could that be for? "Any more news yet?" She asked.

"Not that I am aware of." He said. He sat next to her putting his arm around her.

Reggie stood and stretched.

"I'm going crazy having to stay here when I could be out helping."

That evening they were watching the news. TJ's exclusive story was being reported while they watched. He had covered all the angles and the reward money was mentioned again with a phone number to call with any information. The number flashed up on the screen several times.

"TJ, you did a great job with reporting the whole situation with no sensationalism as Sheriff Johnson would say." Reggie smiled.

The next story caught Reggie's attention right away when TJ had gone into the kitchen.

The reporter said, "The Jenkins Foundation will be holding a dedication ceremony this Friday for the newly constructed outdoor amphitheater and park complete with walking trails, fountains and picnic areas."

"The Jenkins Foundation?" She said out loud as TJ walked back into the room.

"Were they reporting about the dedication ceremony?" He asked as he sat next to her. Reggie was trying to put the pieces together in her head. This had to be part of his family.

"TJ, The Jenkins Foundation, as in Terrence Jenkins and the Jenkins Cereal Corporation?" She was in disbelief. Her heart was now pounding and she was taking a deep breath.

"Yes, I promised my mother I wouldn't miss it. I am so happy it is finally finished and now we can have a little more green space in Chicago for families to enjoy. They can see concerts, picnic and walk the trails. I can't wait to see the finished product."

"I had no idea that was your family. Why haven't you mentioned this to me?" For a moment there was silence between them.

"I was actually going to tell you soon, it just hadn't come up in conversation yet. I wanted you to see me for who I am, not from where I come from. I didn't want my family's wealth to define me and overshadow everything else. I love being a reporter and a writer, which my wife never understood."

"I just wish you had told me sooner", she sighed.

"Please don't let this change how you see me, I'm still the same person you've come to know and care about." His eyes fixated on her. She realized if she had known, she probably would have treated him differently.

"Isn't your father a surgeon? I have read about his philanthropy as well. He was a big contributor to the new hospital, wasn't he?"

"Yes, Reggie, I have an idea, why don't you go with me to Chicago for this dedication coming up?" he beamed with excitement.

"Oh no, I don't think I can do that,"

"Reggie, this would be a great time for you to take a few days off from work. I can take care of all the travel plans for you." he said. I'm sure he can take care of the travel plans, he is loaded, she thought.

"You don't have to answer right now but please think about it", he said as he stood and kissed her forehead as he went into the kitchen.

Oh my goodness, he is TJ Jenkins from THE JENKINS FAMILY. Go to Chicago and meet his family, I'm not sure I'm ready for that. I know I'm not ready.

Reggie called Ed to ask if there were any new developments.

"Nothing as far as Rum yet but they are still at his home. I did get Freddie's cell phone information - the texts from his brothers are all being reviewed by the FBI. Apparently, his brothers had shipments going out on the trains too."

"So, they were all using Freddie and manipulating him because of his job at the port." Her voice was raised. She walked out on the back porch and lit a cigarette.

"He must have refused to do something for them too and that's why they beat him up, "I'm coming back to work in the morning. I will see you then, thanks Ed."

She couldn't get the image out of her head of Freddie being dead at the foot of her driveway. How could she have prevented that from happening? He must have wanted to get out of his situation so badly that he didn't see any other way out. His brothers and Rum Mason will go to jail. How could she even think about going to Chicago at a time like this? She would just have to say, No.

CHAPTER 22

"Reggie, we got some news", Ed said as he walked into her office with a piece of pie and some coffee for her. "Freddie's text with his brothers shows that they were using the drones to distract the inspectors. They were shipping something in their logs that were being loaded onto the trains. We suspect cocaine."

"Any suspicion they were working with Rum and have something to do with these missing girls?" she asked.

"No, so far it looks like they were only shipping something out in their logs." Ed replied and added, "Rum's house had been thoroughly cleaned, no signs of anyone being there.

"I need to talk with Sheriff Johnson, the FBI can't just shut me out of this investigation, I know I can help them." Reggie said as she took a bite of pie, "Delicious."

Ed smiled.

"Oh, I guess you can never have too much pie," TJ said as he put the pie he had just purchased for Reggie on the desk.

Reggie laughed. "One is for breakfast, the other for lunch." Ed glanced up at TJ still standing by the desk.

"How long are you staying here in Birch Creek?" Ed asked.

"Have I worn out my welcome?" TJ smiled, "as a matter of fact, I need to go back to Chicago tomorrow. Reggie, have you thought more about going?"

I can't believe he just asked me that in front of Ed. She shook her head no. "You mean Reggie went with you to Chicago? Why?"

Reggie just stared at TJ. Awkward silence filled the room.

After Ed left the room, TJ asked, "Did I say something wrong?" "Yes, You did."

"You don't want Ed to know that I invited you to go with me to Chicago for the dedication ceremony?"

"That's right."

"Why not?" He was clenching his jaw.

"No one needs to know that you invited me. I'm not going. I can't."

"Reggie, if you haven't noticed, Ed knows we have feelings between us, he sees it." "Do you have feelings for him?" He asked.

"Ed?" She shook her head no. "What do we have? You have a wife, You are a member of the Jenkins family in Chicago, I'm just a damn cowgirl from Birch Creek." Reggie said as she could feel her face getting flushed.

"You go to Chicago, I'm not going." She shouted.

"By the way, she's my ex-wife now." He said as he walked out of her office.

She closed her eyes and took a deep breath.

TJ knew he needed to give her some time to think about what he had said. Ex-wife, sounded so good to him. I didn't handle that well, he thought. He was so glad his attorney had taken care of getting the divorce finalized so quickly and he was sure his ex-wife was too.

TJ knew Ed more than likely had a crush on Reggie. They have worked together for a long time and who wouldn't?, he thought.

Reggie was more anxious now that she knew Rum was behind all of this. She has to help solve this.

"Sheriff Johnson, I started this investigation and they can't just shut me out." Reggie said as she entered his office.

"Shut my door," he said. "Continue to do what you do."

"I won't be told that I'm interfering with their investigation? Hell, listen to what I just said, interfere with THEIR investigation, it's my investigation," she said.

"I need you to listen to me, It's our investigation, meaning all of us. You do your job and let the FBI do theirs. You just experienced a tragedy, you may want to take a day or 2 off. You have been working hard." He said.

Reggie rolled her eyes.

"You sound like somebody else I know, telling me to take time off. I can't and you know exactly what it feels like when a crime hasn't been solved yet." Reggie replied.

Sheriff Johnson has a cold case that he has never been able to solve from at least 15 years ago. It haunted him for years and probably still creeps up in his mind from time to time. Reggie has gone over the case file herself and couldn't find anything else that wasn't done on the case. Sheriff Johnson did everything right.

"Understood." Focus on Freddie's brother's right now. Call them in for an interview. I will let the FBI know we are handling them. It is potentially a local, separate crime, so we have jurisdiction."

"Thank you, I can do that." Reggie nodded her head in appreciation.

Sheriff Johnson always seemed calm, nothing really got him too upset. He was wise and experienced. Reggie respects him so much and worries about the day he decides to retire.

Ed showed Reggie some of the text messages from Freddie's phone to help prepare her for the interview with Phil and Simon.

"I have these texts and I have the photo of the drone in the back of their truck. I also have Captain Joe who saw the drones on several occasions. I need some statements from the Port inspectors too about the drones." Reggie said as she waved bye to Ed while walking out the door.

On her way to the Port, she passed by Freddie's trailer. She wondered about his dog. Did someone take care of it? She would ask if the dog was there when the FBI searched it. Freddie may have been more compassionate than what she previously thought. She now understands Freddie was under a lot of pressure from his brothers and Rum Mason. She wished she could have talked with him more and helped him through this.

The Port was busy today with trucks coming in and out. Michael was at the guard gate. "Hi, Michael." Reggie smiled at him.

"A vision of beauty right before my eyes," he said. Reggie laughed. "I'm sure you use that line on all the women."

"No, just you. What can I help you with today?"

"I wanted to hear what the inspectors said about seeing drones on several occasions."

"Yes, I got each of them to write their own statements about drones. I have them right here for you to review. They confirmed seeing them and also confirmed that it was always when Freddie was working. Poor Freddie, I couldn't believe it when I heard the news." Michael said.

"Did they give any other information?" Reggie asked.

"They said the drones would fly over for approximately 5 minutes each time hovering over the inspection area. I have their contact information for you," he said as he handed her a list.

"Thanks Michael," Reggie backed out of the entrance area making room for a truck coming through the gate.

TJ was waiting for Reggie to come back to the office. He needed to leave this afternoon to go back to Chicago. His father called asking him to come meet with him and their attorney. He didn't want to leave her, he wanted Reggie to go with him. When she walked in her office, she jumped and yelled.

"Damn, you did it again," she said.

"I need to go back to Chicago today. I really wish you would go with me, this is important." Reggie was already shaking her head no before the words came out of her mouth.

"Sorry, TJ, I can't go."

"You can't or you won't?" he asked. She stared at him for a moment and then sat down. "Both." she said.

He wasn't going to push because he was thinking she must not feel the same for him as he does for her. He wanted her to see where he lived, meet his family and see his hometown. This was important to him.

"Alright, I have to go to a meeting with my father and our attorney this afternoon. I guess this is goodbye for now, Reggie."

He gave her that look again. He wanted to hold her and kiss her but he didn't walk towards her. He felt his heart beating, was it breaking? Maybe, he thought..

Reggie had her eyes closed rubbing her temples when Ed walked in. She just let TJ leave with those sad eyes staring at her. What was she thinking? Who am I to turn down a handsome, wealthy, wonderful man like that?

"Are you ok?" Ed asked.

"Yes, I guess, I don't know, just confused about some things"

"TJ?" he smiled. "It's obvious you like him and very obvious he likes you." Reggie had known Ed for a long time and guessed she should confide in him.

"TJ Jenkins, investigative reporter from Chicago is part of the Jenkins family, as in the Jenkins Cereal Corporation and Dr. Jenkins, the famous surgeon," she said.

"My oh my, I had no idea." Ed said.

He was already looking up all the information on the Jenkins family while she told him about the news story she watched about the dedication.

"He wanted me to attend the dedication with him. Can you imagine me attending the dedication with him, it's just ridiculous."

"Why do you think that is ridiculous?"

"Well, it's kind of obvious. Southern country girl who wears a cowboy hat and boots everyday and eats gummy bears and pie for breakfast. Oh and don't forget, smokes cigarettes whenever she can. Damn, I'm a redneck." She proclaimed. "A redneck who cusses and can't solve crimes either." She was on a roll now, just criticizing herself.

"Regina Ann Memphis, any man would love to have you standing by his side at a family dedication ceremony. I think you are scared."

He raised his eyebrows to see what her reaction would be.

"I am scared of embarrassing him. Plus, I have to work on Freddie's brother's investigation." "Get a grip on yourself, Reggie. This is an opportunity for you. You like him, he likes you.

Get out of this town for a couple of days and go see Chicago."

"One other thing I forgot to mention, he is very newly divorced." She responded. "That's a plus that he's not married."

Ed wasn't going to let her continue to make excuses.

"Besides, I wouldn't have any clothes to wear." She looked up making a last ditch effort to make him agree with her.

"Go buy some clothes."

He walked out of her office at this point. She knew he didn't want to hear her make excuses. She grabbed her pack of cigarettes and went outside. She needed to think. She was scared. Scared to go to Chicago, scared she wasn't going to solve this crime, scared these girls weren't going to be found. She had to talk with the Sheriff.

"I need a deputy to go with me up to the logging yard. I want to tell Freddie's brothers to come here for an interview." She said to Sheriff Johnson. "If I try to call them, they may avoid me."

"I will have a deputy go and retrieve them for you. No need for you to go up there."

The deputy brought them into the interview room about an hour later. Reggie was already sitting in there when they walked in. The deputy stayed in the room.

"Some nerve you have sitting here to interview us after you caused our brother to kill himself." Phil yelled.

Reggie was silent.

"What's this all about, Detective Memphis?" Simon asked.

Reggie then asked the deputy to escort Phil out of the room while she talked to Simon. Phil was red faced and cussing.

"We have information about your shipments going out on the trains. We also know about drones."

She leaned in, paused for a few seconds to see if she could get a reaction. "We know what you have been doing,"

Simon was sitting still in the chair, no expression, poker faced.

"We own a logging company, we send logs out as shipments. We have drones that we like to fly over the port just to mess with our brother, of course, we can't do that anymore."

"I believe what you said is only half true. You were using your brother, rather forcing your brother to do illegal shipments. The drones were to distract the inspectors, isn't that right?" Reggie asked.

"Detective Memphis, you're living in some sort of fantasy world. We ship logs, that's it." His voice was monotone, calm and sort of creepy, she thought.

"I know you beat Freddie up because he wouldn't do the illegal shipments anymore, so you were mad. It cuts down on your cash flow."

"Fantasy Island, where's the plane?" He laughed.

"Stay seated, I'll be right back." Reggie went into the room where Ed was watching the interview. "Tell me some of the text messages so I can repeat them to him."

"Look at him, Reggie. He isn't so calm now once you left the room. He is shaking his leg like nobody's business."

Ed was right, Reggie was getting to him. Ed pointed to some of the printouts of their text messages.

"Repeat some of his threats he made to Freddie."

As Reggie walked back in the room, She raised her voice.

"You're just like your daddy, aren't you little brother? Drug addict, piece of shit. You can't do anything right. You better do it, we have to make our quota."

Simon sat staring at her.

"This interview is over, I want an attorney. Don't even try to talk to Phil, he wants an attorney too."

"Phil will have to answer for himself." Reggie said. "You're excused." Simon walked out of the interview looking for Phil.

"Deputy, can you please escort Simon out of the building?" Reggie nodded over to the deputy.

"Of course. Walk this way, please," he said to Simon.

The other deputy had Phil in the back room waiting to be interviewed. Phil was escorted into the interview room. His face was red.

"I"m going to cut to the chase, here." Reggie said. "We know what you and your brother have been doing with the illegal shipments and the drone activity. We also know about the conversations you had with Freddie, including threats you made to him and beating him up when he refused to cooperate." Reggie stared at Phil. She could see Phil clenching his jaw and his face getting more red.

"I don't have any fucking idea what your talking about, Detective. You're just a woman who wants to pretend to do a man's job." he shouted.

"I can refer back to some of the text messages and read them to you, if you like?" She glared.

His phone vibrated on the table. He glanced at it and said, "this interview is over. I want an attorney."

Damn, Simon had texted him.

"Let me escort you out of the building." she said. She knew at this point she didn't have concrete evidence of what they were shipping but knew it was more than just logs.

Reggie asked the Sheriff and Ed to meet with her in the conference room, she remembered something Freddie told her.

"Freddie told me that Rum bought him that truck. It was his payment for doing what he did to Kendra. We need to find out where it was bought and who's name it's in. This will link Rum to Freddie. Can we please call his attorney and demand he come in for questioning?" She asked. Sheriff Johnson asked Ed to do some research on the truck.

"Once we find out more information, then you can call the attorney." Sheriff Johnson replied and held his hand up. "Wait, the FBI needs to be updated and we need a go ahead from them. We have to work together on this." He said sternly looking at Reggie.

"Understood, I don't care who does what, we just need to get that son of a bitch." Reggie uttered.

The lead FBI agent was briefed by Sheriff Johnson. Their analyst will find out everything about Freddie's Toyota truck. The FBI said they don't have to go through Rum's attorney, he can't interfere with a federal investigation. They will find him and bring him in for questioning.

CHAPTER 23

TJ's father sent their private jet to pick him up at the airport. TJ was thankful. During his flight back home, he thought about how great it would be if Reggie joined him in Chicago. He would show her around and spoil her for a couple of days but he thought maybe that's not what she wants, He just needs to stay in Chicago. Reggie and the FBI could handle the investigation without him. He would let her know in a few days that he wasn't coming back. His father was waiting in a limousine for him at the "O'Hare airport when he landed.

"TJ, we are going to pick up your mother and go on to the attorney's office from here. Let's get this legal stuff over with so we can enjoy the rest of the evening together."

His father was a very distinguished and handsome man. People were always commenting that he looked like Harry Belafonte. HIs father was flattered and always said he couldn't see the resemblance. They picked up his mother from the Jenkins Foundation office. She was wearing a blue linen dress and a hat today.

"TJ, thank you for coming back home on such short notice, we are glad you are here." she said.

"Me too, mother."

The attorney sat across from them at a large conference table with three stacks of paper laid out in front of him. TJ wasn't sure what this meeting was about after seeing the stacks of paper. He thought he was going to sign legal forms for the new green space park. He looked at his parents. His father stood. Mr. Jenkins began his prepared speech:

"TJ, your mother and I are retiring. We have accomplished all of our career goals and we have been blessed 1,000 times over. I have sold my medical practice for a very fair price, we closed on it yesterday. I have given your sisters the money from the sale of my practice. Your sisters will now be the owners of The Jenkins Foundation too. They have agreed to continue with projects to better the community. The Jenkins Cereal Corporation is being given to you." He paused for a moment looking at TJ.

Is this real right now? He thought. What the hell is happening?, he felt nauseous.

"You are free to run it as the new owner and CEO or you can sell it, whatever you wish." His father said as he smiled at his wife.

TJ's mother spoke up, "Honey, we don't need anymore than what we already have been given. I will be giving some jewels to your sisters too. I don't need so many now that I will be retired. Your father and I want to travel and enjoy ourselves. We don't want our children to worry over money or worry over us. Please say you accept this gift."

TJ sat staring out the window of the high rise building in downtown Chicago.

"I really don't know what to say. I know nothing about running a major cereal corporation. I can't even begin to know what it's worth."

TJ's father spoke up, "We have all the financial statements right here. We know what it's worth. Sell if you want to. You will have a team of attorneys and a team of financial advisors working to help you make the best investments and sell for the best price, if you so choose."

"What about the Jenkins legacy?" He had tears in his eyes.

"We have all agreed, including your sisters, that it's time for you to either run it or sell it. Our legacy is family, not some factory."

TJ was wiping the tears running down his face.

"You have already given us so much, we already don't have to worry about money, ever." "Well, now you're going to have more." His father laughed. The papers are all right here waiting for each of us to sign.

"I don't know what to say." TJ was wiping the tears again.

"Say yes!" His parents said in unison.

"I will accept your gift but I need time to think about what to do with it." How much time do I have?"

"We are making the announcement after the dedication ceremony on Friday." his father said. "Friday, like in two days? My sisters are ok with Friday?"

TJ was feeling nauseous.

"Yes, they are already planning the next big project." His mother said.

The attorney handed each of them their stack of forms and pens.

"Please provide your signatures where I have each page flagged,"he said.

TJ could hardly sign the pages, his hands were shaking. When they finished, his father said, "Let's go celebrate. Your sisters are at the house waiting for us."

TJ was silent during the car ride to his parents home. He felt as though he may be in shock. This isn't real, this isn't happening. He could not smile, nor cry, nor talk. He needed a drink.

When he walked in the door, his sisters Tasha and Teresa, ran over and hugged him. "Were you as shocked as we were?" Tasha asked him. They were both crying with excitement.

"I'm so glad your divorce is final and that witch doesn't get any of it," Teresa laughed.

"I really need a bourbon," he said. His father poured him a drink and immediately made a toast. TJ knew his father was speaking but the ringing in his ears made it sound muffled. He sat down needing to take it all in. He needed to think in silence. He would stay for the party and then go home and think, possibly all night long.

CHAPTER 24

Reggie was taking a smoke break. This was her time to think. Had she messed up with TJ?

She isn't good enough for him, she thought. She steered her thoughts away from him, she needed to focus. All of sudden she remembered Freddie saying that he refused after Kendra and he tried to stop Myra and Natalie's disappearance. They couldn't have been put in a container car because he was the only one with access. Rum would have used some other form of transportation to get them to where he wanted them to go. She threw her cigarette down and ran inside.

"Sheriff Johnson, those girls weren't put on the train. I remember what Freddie said and it doesn't make sense for us to be looking on trains for them. Rum owns and is CEO of China Tech. He would have his own private plane, I would imagine."

Sheriff Johnson yelled for Ed to come into his office. Reggie explained her revelation to Ed. "That's easy to find out," he said. "I can get the FBI to get all the flight data. We can track his plane. Reggie you're the best." He smiled at her.

Within two hours, they knew about his private jet and where he had traveled in the last 6 months. He made several frequent trips to Nassau in the Bahamas. Ed was working alongside the FBI to uncover all they could about his travels and where he stayed, for how long, etc.

Everywhere he traveled, he was competing in some type of extreme sports events except when he traveled frequently to the Bahamas. Rum had all sorts of photos of where and what he was doing in all the places he traveled. No photos of Rum and Woody together. Woody must have been nothing more than an employee to him.

The FBI analyst found out that Freddie's truck was registered in Freddie's name but it had come from overseas via a shipping container owned by Chinatech. It was shipped to the Savannah port.

"This links Rum to Freddie." Reggie yelled.

"Slow down, it could link them but still not enough evidence to prove anything else." The FBI agent warned.

"We haven't been able to find him yet, so we are reaching out to his attorney to make sure he is aware that we need to question him."

"Reggie, this is going to take a day or two, go do what you know you need to do," Ed said.

She knew what he meant.

She drove to the Country Kitchen. She wanted to eat and talk with Darlene. "Darlene, I need some advice." Reggie said as she walked in the door.

"Well, this calls for me to take a break for the next few minutes. Let me get us something to eat."

Reggie sat for a few minutes. She was twirling her hair around her finger. She never realizes when she does this. She was wondering what TJ was thinking about her, or was he even thinking about her at all? Darlene sat down with 2 cheese burgers.

"Alright, spill the beans, what's going on Regina?" Darlene took a bite of her cheeseburger and leaned closer to hear what Reggie had to tell her.

"TJ the reporter from Chicago is part of the Jenkins Corporation family, you know the cereal company?" She looked at Darlene.

Darlene almost spit her burger out of her mouth. She took a sip of iced tea before speaking. "I could tell he was a special man. Okay, so go on," she said.

"The Jenkins Foundation is having a dedication on Friday for a new green spacepark they have built in downtown Chicago. TJ is very happy and excited about it. He has already gone back to Chicago, he promised his parents he would be there."

"That sounds nice."

"It is very nice and he wanted me to go back to Chicago with him. He invited me to the dedication. I said no and he left."

"Reggie, what in the hell is wrong with you? Why didn't you go?"

"I didn't feel right leaving now during this investigation. I didn't want to embarrass him, I have nothing to wear, I'm a white country cowgirl. Do I need to continue?" She asked.

"He wanted you to come to the dedication with him, not move to Chicago. If he thought you would embarrass him, he wouldn't have invited you, you can buy something to wear and you are a beautiful girl who happens to live in a southern town."

Darlene wasn't going to let her give anymore excuses. Reggie took a bite of her cheeseburger. "You sound just like Ed," Reggie said.

"This is a great opportunity for you to go see Chicago and spend time with that handsome, sweet man who happens to be very wealthy. I really don't want to hear excuses." Darlene pointed at her.

"Well, it may be too late now. He seemed upset with me when he left and I'm not sure he still wants me to go. I haven't heard from him since he left."

"Eat your food and then go outside and call him." Darlene said. "My break time is over, I need to get back to work."

"Thank you for listening to me Darlene."

"Go shopping for a nice summer sundress and cute sandals. You will look gorgeous." Darlene said as she stood cleaning up her dinner plate. Reggie nodded yes.

"Detective Memphis, so good to see you." Reggie heard a familiar voice coming up behind her. When she turned around, she couldn't believe it. She stood up.

"Kendra, I am so glad to see you." Reggie hugged her.

"It's great to see you too." Kendra looked frail but much better than the last time Reggie saw her.

"Here sit here with me. Do you want some pie? I can order you whatever you want, let me buy you some food." Reggie motioned for Darlene to come see Kendra.

"What a day this has turned out to be. All sorts of good things are happening." Darlene smiled.

"How are you feeling? Are you here alone?" Reggie asked.

"Aunt Doris is outside talking nonstop to someone she knows. It is too hot for me to stand out there. She will be here in a minute."

Reggie could see the marks still remained on Kendra's arms, face and neck but she was healing.

"Detective Memphis, I was afraid to come back to Birch Creek but when I heard about Freddie killing himself, I felt more safe. That probably sounds bad to say," she said.

"I understand. When you feel like talking about it, I am here for you, okay?" "I know." Kendra said as her aunt Doris joined them.

"Now, let's put some meat back on Kendra's bones." Doris grinned. Doris was so happy that Kendra was back at home safe. If it hadn't been for Doris calling the Chicago news and making that giant poster of Kendra, she might still be in the hospital trying to heal. Reggie knew that when someone has a family who loves them, it helps them to heal. As Reggie finished her food and paid for their meals, she reminded Kendra to stay in touch and call her whenever she felt like it.

"I have to get going now." Reggie waved bye to Darlene. Darlene held up her fingers to her ear as if she was holding a phone, signaling Reggie to make that phone call. Reggie laughed.

Kendra was replaying the events over and over in her head. She may be healing but not emotionally. She didn't want to go out to eat today but her Aunt wanted her to eat some good country cooking and celebrate being at home. Kendra smiled and nodded at the people who stopped by their booth to say hello and welcome her home. She knew her life had changed now. She wanted to help find the other girls but wasn't sure what to do. The only

2 people that she knew were in on her kidnapping were both now dead. She was feeling guilty that she was ok now but the other girls had not been found. She couldn't help but wonder what would have happened had those men not heard her fighting with Woody. Where would she be now?

Reggie didn't try to call TJ until she got in her soft bed that evening. Sammy lay at her feet. He didn't answer her call. She has truly messed up what could be a wonderful time in Chicago and possibly more than a friendship. She could text him, she thought. No, wait to see if he calls back. I'm going to book a flight to Chicago and show up in my sundress with my southern accent, boots and cowboy hat. She shook her head at the thoughts of it.

CHAPTER 25

TJ got back to his penthouse after his family's celebration. The silence was good. The soft glow of city lights cast a warm ambiance over his penthouse. His life has just drastically changed. He had changed from being wealthy to now being a billionaire within a few hours. The weight of the world seemed to rest on his shoulders even though it was a wonderful feeling and opportunity to have been given this gift. He knew it was an enormous decision he was having to make. Why had he not ever thought about the day his parents would retire? It had not crossed his mind they would retire soon and leave the company to him. His head was spinning. The news of his inheritance was a shock. It was a legacy he never expected nor desired and the weight of it all seemed threatening to him. He looked at his phone. Missed call. Reggie had called him. He smiled at seeing her name on his phone. He couldn't talk to her right now. He had to sort all of this out. Alone in the silence, he sat on his plush leather sofa with his mind swirling with a whirlwind of emotions. On one hand, the prospect of selling the company was tempting, a chance to free himself of the burden of expectation and create his own future. But on the other hand, it was a decision that carried such immense weight and consequences both for himself and the employees of the Jenkins Corporation. These employees depended on the company for their livelihood.

TJ stood up at the windows looking out at the night skyline, he was lost in thought. He started thinking about questions he never really asked himself. Questions about his identity and making his own path, his purpose and what does success look like to him?

Hours had passed without him realizing the time due to his mind spinning with a million different scenarios and possibilities. It was a decision that would shape the course of the rest of his life, he knew he wanted to consider all options.

As the sun began to rise, TJ had been up all night. He stood up from the sofa and told himself it was a new day. He would rise to the challenge of making this tough decision and embrace all the consequences it may bring. He has a team of attorneys and financial advisors who will meet with him and advise as he makes decisions. His decision was made, he would sell with stipulations. He wanted to ensure the well-being of the company's employees would be protected. He would ask his team to meticulously craft a set of stipulations to be included in the sale agreement. He wanted the employees to be given the option to stay on with the new ownership if they so choose. For those who preferred to leave or retire, he would offer severance packages or retirement options.

He would call his parents this morning to tell them his decision and then call his attorney and financial advisors to start working on the sales agreements. He was already feeling optimistic about his future and really wanted to share all of this news with one person, Reggie.

CHAPTER 26

Rum had not been on social media for several days. Nick was re-decorating the Italian villa in case it was their new permanent home. Nick Daniels was an interior decorator and wedding/party planner. He loved all things social. It was hard on him to try to stay hidden. Rum met NIck at a party in Paris. Nick had been the party planner for that night's spectacular event.

Rum knew Nick was the person he wanted to spend the rest of his life with very shortly after meeting him. Rum always knew he was gay, even in the Navy, especially in the Navy. He hated women. Carla Montgomery made fun of him in high school and told everyone about how he couldn't get it up when she stripped down naked and climbed on top of him. She was the person who pushed him over the edge that he had been teetering on for a while. He didn't feel guilty about what he did to her the next summer. She had it coming. He remembers that she didn't return to school that next year. Women were sluts who meant nothing to him. He never felt the slightest shame for selling them now. Rum knew that Nick pretended to not know that Rum was managing the biggest trafficking ring in the world. Nick was smarter than he let on. Rum had spoiled Nick with their luxurious lifestyle and he knew Nick would never give that up.

Rum was getting restless and he knew Nick was too. Italy was providing a great sanctuary for them temporarily but the adrenaline junkie within him carved the rush of some danger and excitement that only the extreme sports that he had come to love could provide. He started searching on his laptop for the next thrill and then he found it. A cliff diving competition in Greece.

"Nick, how about we take a trip to Greece and I will enter this cliff diving competition?" Rum was excited about this news. He had been in several cliff diving competitions before, he definitely wasn't the best but he would never discuss not winning.

Nick raised up from his seat.

"Greece, really? I thought we needed to lay low for a while." Nick uttered.

"I need a break and what better way to get the adrenaline going than cliff diving." "You can count me in." Nick agreed. "You have to remember that we can't draw any unnecessary attention to ourselves so don't go and win the competition." He smiled.

"I know what I'm doing, the feds can't connect me with any of this, there is no evidence." Rum booked the trip with a few clicks of the buttons on his laptop.

"I will make sure everything goes as planned and besides, what's life without a little risk?" Rum smiled. "Don't worry."

A new email popped up on Rum's laptop from his attorney.

It read: *"I have been trying to contact you. You need to call me when you read this message."*

Rum called right away, "what it is?"

"Rum, The FBI says they need to question you. You will have to comply with their federal investigation. I can sit with you during the interview. I need you to tell me why they are wanting to question you - you have to level with me."

"I don't know why they want to question me, that damn detective Memphis has put some ideas in their head. There isn't anything to link me to the crimes they are investigating." Rum was yelling at this point.

"Well, we will have to just wait and see what questions they ask you. I will try to find out how soon you need to be interviewed."

"Alright, thanks." Rum said disconnecting the call. "You look worried, what is wrong?" Nick asked Rum.

"No, I'm not worried, just pissed off. The feds want to question me. My attorney said I have to comply." Rum rolled his eyes.

"You will be amazing and you will no longer be a suspect once they interview you." Nick smiled.

CHAPTER 27

Kendra lay awake, wanting to call Detective Memphis. The nights were long and her bedroom seemed scary and too dark. The container car had been pitch black at night and she always heard what sounded like mice in the car with her. Since being at her mom's house, she started keeping her light on at night. She had not been able to sleep since she awoke from her coma. Everything was playing over and over in her mind. Freddie was her friend for years, they grew up together. She knew he had a bad reputation for stealing and doing drugs but drugging her and kidnapping her? Why? Why me? Who made him do this? And that man, Woody, would come in and give me water and a sandwich and then leave again. What was he going to do with me? Why did I have to wear that wrist band? She had so many unanswered questions but she also knew what the FBI had told her. They think the plan was for her to be put on a ship and shipped to another country and be sold or trafficked. The tears kept coming as she wiped her face. Freddie and that man, Woody are both dead, that seemed so weird to her, why? She hasn't been able to express her feelings to anyone. She has talked with her best friend, Shay and her mother and Aunt Doris but they just hug her and ask questions. She knows she needs to talk with a therapist. When she does fall asleep, it's a nightmare about being tied up and handcuffed. She is thankful the ICU nurse identified her and she wasn't sure how to express her gratitude. She was thankful he received some award money. She meant to ask Detective Memphis who was the person responsible for giving him that money.

CHAPTER 28

Reggie made up her mind to take the advice of her friends. She was going to Chicago.

She took a deep breath and called TJ. No answer.

She texted: "TJ, I am coming to Chicago today. I am sorry for not making this decision sooner. I miss you."

As she was looking up flights her phone rang, it was TJ.

"Reggie, I miss you. I'm so happy you are coming. Let me make arrangements for your flight on our private plane. I will meet you at the airport."

"Private plane?" She was stunned. "Yes, Can you be ready to go by noon?"

Reggie was trying to picture herself on a private jet.

"Yes, but I have no idea where to go once I reach the airport."

"I will have a car pick you up at your house and take you straight to board the plane. I will let you know what time the car will arrive."

"Okay." She agreed because she was still too shocked to say anything else. After she hung up she sat on her bed taking some deep breaths. Damn, she thought. I need something to wear to the dedication.

She texted TJ: *"I forgot, I need to go shopping for a dress for the dedication."*

He responded: *"We can go when I pick you up at the airport."* *"Wow, you have an answer for everything. Ok"* she responded.

She notified Sheriff Johnson and Ed that she was taking a couple of days off. Ed would feed Sammy while she was gone. She stepped out on her back porch to smoke one last cigarette, her last one ever.

TJ made all the arrangements. He wanted everything to be perfect for Reggie. He ordered groceries to be delivered including some gummy bears. He called his parents to tell them his decision to sell. After all these years of a family business, they seemed happy about his decision. Maybe they wanted all of that behind them now. He had an overwhelming sense of freedom, weight had been lifted from him. He would quit his job, he would write, he was happy.

Reggie was twirling her finger in her hair in the limousine on her way to the airport. She had never been in a car like this. She felt proud and important as people in the passing cars were looking in the back tinted windows wanting to see who was inside. She pulled at her skirt that seemed shorter than she remembered. She was wearing a floral silk blouse and a white skirt with sandals with a slight heel. She also had on a pair of her grandmother's diamond earrings that she has always cherished. She pulled her hair up in a loose bun because it was another extremely hot day. Her hair was long and thick and made her sweat. She left her cowboy boots and hat at home.

The limo pulled into a private plane hangar area. The driver parked, got out and opened her door.

"Is this the plane I'm supposed to board?" she asked.

"Yes, ma'am it is. I will load your luggage."

She was trying to hand him a tip, he held his hand up and said that it was already taken care of. She felt relieved as to not embarrass herself by not tipping enough. She was greeted by the pilot and a flight attendant. When she entered the plane, it was unlike any plane she had ever seen. The cabin area had nice wide leather seats. She counted 8 seats total. The flight attendant was there for her needs and her needs only. No one else was boarding the plane.

Wow, she thought, this is how the wealthy people live. She was not in need of any food or drinks, blanket or pillow. The flight attendant was really not needed for her. She felt guilty for not ordering anything so she decided to ask for champagne, that would help calm her nerves. She ended up having 2 glasses.

When the plane landed, she saw another limo parked as she looked out the window.

She watched Mr. TJ Jenkins step out to greet her. Now, she could see that he was in his element. He belonged here with the fancy plane, limo's, clothes and city life. She took a couple of deep breaths wishing she had a cigarette to calm her nerves. I can do this, she thought. TJ ran up the stairs to the door of the plane. He was smiling so big, showing that cute dimple.

He hugged her, thanked the crew and said, "Let's go."

He had wine waiting for her in the car with some cheese and grapes. "I thought you might be hungry. How was your flight?" he asked.

"Do you even have to ask? It was incredible, thank you so much for all of this."

Reggie was overwhelmed by the private plane, limos and the city. She felt like a country girl who wasn't sure what to do in the city. TJ was the perfect host, making her feel welcomed. She could tell he was very sincere in making her feel comfortable and knew he was excited for her to see Chicago. Reggie reminded him that she needed to go shopping to pick out a new dress to wear to the dedication. She was hesitant about where to shop and could she afford any of the dresses? It was as if he was reading her mind.

"Reggie, I can take you to some shops downtown or wherever you would like to shop. I can also have someone bring some dresses to my place for you to try on. Just tell me what you want to do."

"You can have someone bring some dresses to your place for me to try on? Are you serious? I doubt I could afford any that would be brought to your home."

Reggie was realizing that TJ is used to a pampered life even though he never presents himself that way. She was getting more nervous about being there each minute that passed.

"You are my guest, I invited you to join me so I will be purchasing your dress," He told the driver to take them to his place.

"Reggie, I want you to enjoy this trip, you deserve it. Please don't argue with me about purchasing a dress for you. It's not a big deal."

Reggie knew she would rather try on some dresses at his home because she wouldn't feel as intimidated by some expensive boutique.

"Ok."

They drove into a parking garage where the driver let them out at a private elevator with a special keypad. This was his private elevator that led to the penthouse. The elevator was glass on the inside and took them all the way up to the 45th floor. She could see lots of the city from inside the elevator.

"What a spectacular view," she sighed.

As the doors opened, Reggie could see huge windows all around. The entrance foyer was luxurious with a warm glow, not too elegant but beautiful. The view was breathtaking. TJ showed her around. The living room was equally as elegant and warm with soft light and leather sofas arranged all around a glass coffee table. A beautiful fireplace aligned one wall. A beautiful cityscape painting was above the fireplace. She turned towards the sleek modern kitchen with a large marble island that seemed to be the focal point of the kitchen. A bottle of wine and two glasses stood waiting on the countertop for them. TJ showed her the bedrooms with their plush linens and luxurious curtains that were tied open showing the gorgeous windows and awesome views. The adjacent bathrooms were the most elegant bathrooms she had ever seen. The bathtub in his bathroom was a deep copper tub with copper fixtures. The shower was just as lovely with the italian tile and the large rain shower nozzle that lookedlike art work hanging down.

TJ asked her to join him in the living room. He wanted to enjoy some wine and talk about the last 24 hours. He couldn't wait to share the news with her. As she walked back into the living room, she was immediately drawn again to the spectacular view. She walked out onto the terrace. It was beautiful with tropical looking house plants.

"Someone has a green thumb, I see." she smiled.

"Not me, I have someone who takes care of these plants for me."

TJ looked like he was embarrassed to admit it. They walked back inside and sat down together. "Does your family know I am here and coming to the dedication ceremony?"

"Not yet." He knew they would be so glad it wasn't his ex-wife attending. "I hope they won't think I am intruding." She raised her eyebrows.

"Of course not." TJ said.

"I have to tell you what has happened in the last 24 hours to me. It's a whole lot to process and I'm not really even sure I have processed it yet. I was awake all night and haven't even gone to bed."

"Wow, it must be something either really bothering you or you're so excited you can't sleep?" TJ took a deep breath and let it out slowly.

"I am now the owner of the Jenkins Corporation." Reggie's mouth literally fell open.

"What?" "How?"

This news was just as surprising as when she found out he was from the Jenkins Family. She was stunned and just stared at him.

"I am the owner, my parents have given permission for me to sell it if I choose to not be the CEO."

Reggie was having a hard time comprehending it all.

"When do you take over, what does this mean about your job at the news station?" Reggie had so many questions, she couldn't think straight.

"I stayed up all night weighing all options and I'm choosing to sell it." TJ was smiling and seemed confident in his decision.

"My parents have now retired as of yesterday. My sisters will be running the foundation and working on the philanthropic side of things. I have quit my job at the news station and now I can write books." He beamed with excitement.

"TJ, I am at a loss for words, I truly don't know what to say except, Congratulations! I am so proud of you and your family."

"I couldn't wait to share this news with you. You don't know how relieved I am that you decided to come here."

"This calls for a big celebration." Reggie announced.

Right after she said it, the intercom chimed. The dresses have arrived for Reggie to try on.

Reggie was nervous about trying these on and seeing the prices.

She went into the bedroom where the dresses had been laid out on the bed. They were all beautifully made with luxurious material but not too overdone. Reggie felt like a princess even though they weren't evening gowns, just amazing sundresses. She chose a green floral one with spaghetti straps. It was form fitting and she loved it. No price tags on any of the dresses. She walked out wearing the dress she had chosen to show TJ and made sure it passed the test.

"You look amazing!" TJ's eyes lit up.

"Is this one a good choice for the dedication ceremony?"

"How could it be any better, you are beautiful." TJ said as he hugged her. "I'm so glad you are here."

They decided to stay in that evening and have a quiet celebration. TJ had not slept and the lack of sleep was catching up with him. They drank champagne and TJ grilled steaks and vegetables out on the terrace.

"This has been an unbelievable past couple of days." He said. Shortly after speaking those words, TJ fell asleep on the sofa. Reggie covered him up with a blanket and quietly cleaned up the dishes and went into the guest bedroom. She knew he was exhausted and needed to sleep.

CHAPTER 29

Reggie met TJ's parents and sisters right before the ceremony began. They were very much like what she had pictured in her mind, she had actually seen photos of his parents on TV before but not his sisters. They all looked like wealthy people. They seemed surprised that she was accompanying TJ but were welcoming her with open arms and handshakes. TJ introduced her as Detective Regina Memphis, just so everyone was clear.

"This green space is so beautiful. What a wonderful space for families to come to in the city and have picnics or celebrations. They can walk the trails and see the well manicured landscaping with all kinds of native plants. The added touch of an amazing rose garden with so many varieties of roses, it is so well designed." Reggie said to TJ and his family.

"Well, thank you so much. We can't take credit for the designs but we hope it will bring joy to many people here in the city. It's our way of giving back." Mrs. Jenkins said as she shook Reggie's hand.

The dedication ceremony was completed with a ribbon cutting, speeches given and photos taken. The Chicago News channels were also there covering the story. Reggie didn't feel right standing up on the stage with TJ and his family but he insisted. She felt like a celebrity with all eyes on them and cameras flashing in their faces. TJ had told her she looked so beautiful and he was glad she had accompanied him.

He declined the invitation to have dinner with his family, he wanted to spend time with Reggie.

They walked along the river walk, he held her hand as he explained all of his favorite places in the city. They ate dinner at his favorite Cafe' and then were dropped off at his penthouse elevator.

When they reached the penthouse, the doors opened and the night sky view was incredible. He turned to her and they kissed. She took off her heels and needed to sit down due to feeling lightheaded. She leaned over when he sat beside her and kissed him again. She wasn't going to stop him if he wanted more. She knew she wanted more. He picked her up and carried her to his bedroom. He slowly undressed her and then took his clothes off. Her body was tingling as he pressed against her. He was taking his time, kissing all over her body. She found him irresistible and wanted to feel him inside her. TJ was an incredible lover, wanting to satisfy her like she had never felt before. He made love to her several times throughout the night. Reggie had never had such an incredible experience, he was everything she everwanted.

CHAPTER 30

Rum read the New York Times which happened to pick up the story of the Jenkins family dedicating the new green space and Mr. and Mrs. Jenkins retirement. Then he saw it, the photo with the family's names and there she was Detective Regina Memphis in a photo with TJ Jenkins. What in the hell is she doing in this photo? How can she be connected to this family in Chicago? Then on another page of the paper, he read an article about TJ being single but maybe not for long with this gorgeous detective on his arm. Detective Memphis is dating a wealthy bachelor from Chicago? He couldn't believe it was the same Detective Memphis. He checked her photo on the Birch Creek Sheriff's office website just to make sure it was the same person.

Now was his time to strike. Detective Memphis had been a thorn in his side. He made a call to one of his employees and explained what he wanted to happen in Birch Creek while Detective Memphis was in Chicago with her new boyfriend. She needs to learn her lesson to not mess with me. I can destroy her world so she has something else to focus on besides me.

CHAPTER 31

TJ and Reggie were drinking coffee out on his terrace the next morning after the most magical night she had ever had. She was smiling and couldn't help but think about wanting more right then and there on the terrace. Her cell phone rang, It was Sheriff Johnson.

"Good morning, Sheriff." She was surprised to be hearing from him.

"Reggie, I have some bad news." Her heart sank as she listened. "Your house burned last night." His voice was shaking. "The fire department responded right away but they couldn't save it, they thought some sort of explosive was used. Luckily, Ed had taken Sammy to his house yesterday. I am so sorry, Reggie."

She was stunned, she couldn't talk.

"An investigation is underway, the fire chief says some sort of explosive was somehow dropped onto your house, possibly a drone. Freddie's brothers are at the station now being questioned."

"I'm coming home, now." She managed to get the words out but wasn't sure if he understood her because she was almost hyperventilating. She handed the phone to TJ. Sheriff Johnson repeated it again.

"I will take care of her, call me back with any news. We will come to Birch Creek as soon as possible."

Reggie was devastated. Who? Why? How?

TJ arranged the flight, car and everything within a few minutes. They didn't take any clothes or items with them. Reggie stared out the window of the limo wondering if anything was left of her home. She kept saying she was so thankful that Ed had Sammy and she was not at home.

"TJ, what am I going to do? Where will I live? Who did this? Am I safe? Is someone trying to kill me?" Reggie couldn't stop asking questions.

When they drove up to the burnt remains of her home, after staring at the burned parts of the frame that remained standing, she sat down on the grass. The fire investigators and insurance adjusters were talking at the top of the driveway. She wiped her eyes and said, "I am so thankful I was in Chicago with you and that Ed took Sammy to his house. We both could have died." TJ sat down next to her with his arm around her shoulders as she stared at the burnt area that used to be her house.

"Whoever did this wanted to kill me or send me a message. It has to be someone connected to these disappearances."

"The FBI and Sheriff Johnson are handling it." TJ said as he pulled her close, wrapping his arms around her. Yellow tape was outlining the perimeter of the house. Nothing was left, except her jeep was still parked in the driveway, they couldn't get close enough to it to see if it was damaged or not.

"What am I going to do? Where am I going to live?"

"Reggie, you can go back to Chicago with me for a few days and we can sort this out. I am here for you, let me take care of you." TJ stared into her eyes with his hands holding her head.

"You shouldn't have to take care of me."

"I want to, Reggie." He said sternly.

Reggie felt empty, she couldn't think straight. She kept seeing the image of Freddie dead at the bottom of her driveway and now this fire image would remain in her head too.

"TJ, I'm not sure I can deal with all of this right now. We still have to find 2 missing girls. The stress of all of this is weighing on me and makes me feel weak," she said.

"You are not weak Regina. Let me handle some of this for you right now and let the FBI handle their part too."

When they arrived at the Sheriff's office, Ed stood and hugged her. "Sammy is just fine", he said. "I thought it would be easier to just bring him to my house while you were gone so that's what I did."

"Thank God you did, Ed. I am so thankful."

Sheriff Johnson asked Reggie if she felt like talking with the FBI. They had some questions for her. She agreed to speak with Joel, the FBI agent alone in the conference room.

"Reggie, We are holding Freddie's brothers here but so far their alibis check out. A search warrant is being executed of their property and trucks as we speak. I'm told their drones are not the type that can hold and release an object. A more high tech drone is used for dropping explosives. We are definitely not dismissing the fact that they could be involved in this. Did they threaten you at any time?"

"No, they blame me for their brother killing himself. They know we have information on them that could lead to several charges on them."

"Can you tell me who all knew you were going out of town?"

"Yes, Sheriff Johnson, Ed, TJ and Darlene at Country Kitchen. They are the only ones.

Whomever did this may have thought I was at home. My jeep was in the driveway, they may not have known I was out of town. They may have wanted to kill me."

"We can set up security protection for you for the next several days,"

"You don't need to do that. Right now, I have no place here to go, I will return back to Chicago with TJ. HIs building is very secure."

"I want you to stay in touch with me and I will do the same, agree?" Joel asked. "Of course, I will probably bug the hell out of you." She laughed.

TJ, Ed and Sheriff Johnson joined her and Joel back in the conference room. Ed updated her on information they have gathered so far on Rum. He told her they are seeing a pattern of his flights to the Bahamas. They are checking on all his travels and they think he will go back to the Bahamas very soon. They have agents in the Bahamas now doing some surveillance.

"Joel, I just thought of something. You said the drone used at my house was a more high tech drone used to drop explosives." Reggie asked.

"That is what we are currently thinking," he said.

"Rum Mason is the Owner and CEO of China Tech and he is a former military man. His company may make these types of drones?"

"Great observation and thinking Reggie." Sheriff Johnson said. Joel took notes and said he would relay the information ASAP.

Sheriff Johnson stood up and leaned down towards Reggie. "I am giving you a directive and you can't tell me "No" on this one. You will take some time off effective immediately."

He waited on Reggie's reaction.

"I am going to 100% agree with you today." She smiled. "Well that settles that." He said.

Reggie looked over at TJ.

"I will be going back to Chicago with TJ." TJ nodded, yes.

"Reggie, let Sammy stay with me for a few more days until you get settled.?" Ed asked. "If you really don't mind keeping him a few more days that would help me out. Thank you, Ed."

Reggie and TJ flew back to Chicago. She knew Sheriff Johnson and Ed would call her if needed and notify her of any good news. TJ was very comforting towards her and seemed to be one step ahead in knowing what she may need. The only things left that she owned were the items she packed in her suitcase for her trip to Chicago. He wanted her to feel comfortable and he truly wanted to take care of her. He brought her a cup of hot tea when she was sitting out on the terrace.

"TJ, last night was the most magical and best night of my life and today seemed to be the worst day. I'm trying to make sense of it all and how I can go from such ecstasy to such despair. BUT what makes it all better is you." She smiled at him.

"Let's have many more nights like last night, is that a deal?" he asked. "That sounds like an amazing deal to me." Reggie managed a smile.

CHAPTER 32

Rum had received word that his instructions were carried out successfully. Now, maybe that detective can have other things to deal with rather than trying to bug the shit out of me. He thought. He knew his employees were loyal and would not link him to ordering the drone attack at Reggie's home. He didn't care if his team was caught because he had convinced them that they were safe from any prosecution.

Nick rushed in telling Rum about an account he had been offered. He is asked to coordinate and decorate for an upcoming fundraiser party in New York City in a couple of months. He wanted to make sure Rum thought it would be ok for him to travel to New York.

"Of course, you will do a fabulous job." Rum said.

CHAPTER 33

A week had already passed since the fire. Reggie knew she was in love with TJ but hadn't said the words yet to him. She didn't feel it was the right time since she had been going through this trauma. She felt safe and secure with him. Since taking time off, she realized being away from Birch Creek was a good move. She knew the FBI was doing all they could to locate the missing girls and bring criminal charges against Rum. She had talked briefly to Ed and the Sheriff who reported that Freddie's brothers were not responsible for the drone explosive attack. They had been charged with selling and possession of cocaine and several other charges related to transporting it via their logging business. They had bonded out of jail and retained an attorney. They would do jail time according to Sheriff Johnson. Also, The FBI reports Rum has an estate in the Bahamas, it's not listed in his name but they are sure he owns it. They think women are being held captive there and then sent to other countries to be trafficked. No women have been seen yet. They assume this estate is the main location based on the security guards that surround this estate. They continue to do surveillance 24/7.

Reggie was ecstatic that Freddie's brothers were arrested and the FBI was closing in on Rum and finding the girls. She wondered how many other women were being held captive. How many had already been sent overseas and trafficked. She wants to help bring down Rum Mason once these girls are found.

Time is what she has right now - she has lost her home but found love. Love that she has never experienced before. Having TJ during this time has made all the difference for her.

Seeing the bigger picture is much easier now. Time to think about her future. She feels like she can breathe and focus on what's important. Where she will live, will she rebuild her home, will she continue to work for Sheriff Johnson?

TJ saw her sitting and staring, lost in her thoughts. "Reggie, what is it?

"I think I'm overwhelmed with your generosity and knowing I have some tough decisions to make." She pulled away to look at him. "I love you and I don't want you to think I'm taking advantage of you."

"Advantage of me? Please do. I love you too. I want to help you and protect you and give you everything you want out of life. We can tackle those tough decisions together."

She kissed his lips and began kissing his neck. She felt him pull her closer to him. She loved his smell, the feel of his lips on hers and how he holds her head when he kisses her. He began slowly unbuttoning her shirt. She was already feeling a tingling sensation again. They moved into the bedroom. He gently laid her on the bed and began kissing her all over her body. He made love to her with such passion and admiration.

CHAPTER 34

Reggie had received the official investigative report from the fire department. The cause of the fire was an explosive dropped on to her house more likely from a drone. She knew that Rum had to be responsible. He was out to get her for uncovering his operation. She couldn't believe all he has done to these women and how much money he has made with trafficking human beings. She wondered how many people work for him and how many have bought or paid for these girls. He needs to rot in jail along with all the others who have paid him.

She had decided to have her lot cleared and she would sell it. It was a great lot in the downtown area. She didn't want to return to that area. She also had time to think about her career. She wants to continue to work as a detective but work on sex trafficking cases in the future. She will apply for a trafficking unit job possibly here in Chicago. First things first though, she has to get back to work and help solve this case. She was going back to Birch creek today to help with the investigation. Sheriff Johnson's wife had extended an invitation to her to stay with them for a few days. She was thankful for their kindness and felt secure to stay with them.

Everyone at the Sheriff's Department welcomed her back with hugs and bags of gummy bears sitting on her desk. They knew her well and she had already let it leak that she had officially quit smoking. She had a note on her desk from Kendra.

It read: *Detective Memphis, I was so sorry to hear about your house. I am thankful you are ok. I would like to talk to you when you come back to work. Love, Kendra.*

Reggie asked Kendra to meet her at Darlene's so they could eat dinner together. Darlene started crying as soon as Reggie walked into the restaurant.

"Reggie, thank goodness you are here. I have missed you so much. Come stay with me if you need a place to stay." She wiped the tears away and hugged her tight.

"Thank you Darlene, I love you. You are a sweetheart. Right now, I am staying at Sheriff Johnson's house, his wife insisted."

"Kendra is waiting for you in the last booth. We can talk after you meet with her. I will send someone over to take your order in a few minutes,"

Kendra was smiling at the sight of Reggie. She stood up to hug her. Her injuries were almost all healed and she was such a beautiful girl. After they greeted each other, Kendra jumped right in to say what she wanted to tell Reggie.

"I know I'm having PTSD. The trauma from being kidnapped, knowing that Woody was killed after I escaped and then knowing that Freddie killed himself has been hard to comprehend. I'm seeing a counselor weekly but not sure it is helping." Tears ran down her face as she grabbed Reggie's hand.

"I am so sorry you had to go through all of this, Kendra." Reggie squeezed her hand. "Reggie, I want to help others who have gone through a traumatic experience. I feel like maybe I went through and survived to help others."

"Kendra, you could make a huge impact. You are so brave and sharing your story will help other people."

"I have been playing the night with Freddie over and over in my head and I remembered something that I saw at his house. I don't know if it matters now or not, but I thought it was strange."

"What was it, Kendra?"

"When Freddie was making our drinks in his kitchen, I was sitting on his sofa. I saw a box on the table and I opened it. It was a military medal - I remember it read: *"Navy, good conduct."*

It was fancy looking and I remember thinking he probably stole it from somewhere. It just seemed out of place." Kendra looked up at Reggie.

"Kendra, Rum Mason was in the Navy. Freddie could have stolen it from his house. This could help link him with Rum. I will ask the FBI if they found it when they searched Freddie's place. Good work, Kendra." Reggie said as she patted Kendra's hand.

"Let's order some food and dessert!" Reggie smiled.

When Reggie left the restaurant, she called Ed and asked him to look at Rum's social media information to see if he ever posted anything about getting any medals. Ed would look and let her know tomorrow morning.

Reggie met with Sheriff Johnson and Ed to discuss what the FBI may have found at Rum and Freddie's houses during those searches. Sheriff Johnson called agent Reynolds to ask if any medals were seen at either of their homes. Reynolds reported that Rum had a big collection of medals in a bookcase in his home library. They didn't find any type of medal at Freddie's house.

"That medal had to have come from Rum's collection. I bet Freddie stole it and either sold or pawned it. We can check the pawn shop today." Reggie blurted out.

"Yes, you can check the pawn shop, but it doesn't prove it was Rum's unless his name was on it. If we link it to being Rum's medal, it still doesn't prove he was "in business" with Freddie. Freddie could have broken in and stole it from his house." Sheriff Johnson uttered.

"You're right but it could still help us put Freddie in Rum's house."

Agent Reynolds reported, "We will be closing in soon at the Bahamas compound. We are working around the clock with surveillance and data from flights and shipping containers to at least five different countries. We will keep you all updated as we get closer to raiding the compound. Rum has not been seen at the compound, nor has he been seen disembarking from the plane trips to the Bahamas. It could be his plane making the flights but he hasn't been on any of them. Also, his attorney hasn't heard from him nor can we find him to bring him in for questioning.

Reggie lowered her head in disappointment.

"He is a narcissist who may have been smart enough to not link himself to any of this. We have to find the missing pieces that link him as the mastermind." Reggie said as she pounded her fist on the table.

CHAPTER 35

Reggie couldn't believe she was approved to travel with the FBI to the Bahamas. They said she had played such a major part in this investigation, they knew how personal it can become and she needed to continue to work on it until it was solved. She stared out the plane window at the beautiful blue water. They would be at Rum's Bahama's compound within a couple of hours.

The team was strategizing on how to enter his compound. They still had not received confirmation that Rum was there. They had agents watching who was coming and going. Reggie prayed Natalie and Myra would be there. Their families were made aware of this situation and of the possibilities. He could have sent them to another country by now but she knew they were hot on his trail and he would be arrested and the girls would be found.

They were each given protective gear and vests to wear for when they entered the compound. It would happen fast. Reggie was the one who could identify Myra and Natalie. Three FBI swat vans were headed towards the compound. They would park on the east side of the gates and sneak up to the gate. Reggie never felt so ready in her life. She could feel the adrenaline rushing through her body. The first agents blew up the gate, they charged in.

Reggie's first thought was, where are all the people? The guards, the girls? It was silent. They split up into three teams. The first group would enter through the back, the second group through the front. Reggie's group would enter into the front when the signal was given. Her heart was pounding out of her chest. This compound was eerily silent. It didn't look like a lush bahama resort. It was an old stucco spanish style that needed some paint. The windows had bars on them. This had to be where they kept the girls. It had a huge tacky looking fountain out front with a statue of a mermaid. The signal was given. They ran in, Reggie along with her team surged forward, bounding up the spiral staircase and into the dimly lit hallway that stretched before them. Rows of doors, four on each side, each one a potential chamber of horrors. The anguished cries of women echoed through the corridor, a chilling reminder of the suffering within.

Reggie's heart clenched as she took in the sight before her: gaunt figures huddled in their rooms, their bodies emaciated, their spirits broken, shackled to the cruel confines of their beds. Yet amid the despair, a glimmer of hope ignited because help had finally arrived.

It was the 3rd door on the right, Natalie and Myra were together. Reggie moved closer to make sure it was them.

Natalie screamed, "Detective Memphis!"

She held both of them in her arms. She could feel their bones sticking out. They were safe now. "Detective Memphis, How did you find us?" Natalie whispered as though she didn't want the guards to hear.

"A whole team of people have been working around the clock to find you." Reggie answered. "Let's get out of here."

The agents gathered all the girls together to take them all outside to the vans. The guards had all been secured with handcuffs but Rum was nowhere to be found. Reggie stood outside, closed her eyes, the girls were all going home.

There were a total of 40 women rescued. The girls were flown to Miami and each of the girls spent the night in the hospital to be examined. The families were contacted. They ranged in age and where they came from but all were from the United States. All of the women were taken to the Miami FBI headquarters to be interviewed. They all reported more women had been there too but they had been taken away. The FBI knew other women had been sent to other countries and they were working internationally with other jurisdictions to recover them. The FBI allowed Reggie to help interview Myra and Natalie.

Myra was the first of the 2 that Reggie would help interview. Myra was smiling with dark circles under her eyes, her hands were shaking and her arms were like twigs sticking out from an oversized sweatshirt. She was happy to be rescued and going home. Reggie asked that Myra explain what happened to her from the night she was taken until now when rescued. She told her to go slow and take breaks whenever she needed to. Myra nodded in agreement. The FBI agent was going to take notes and record the conversation while Reggie asked the questions.

Myra explained, "I was at the Handy Mart after work buying some snacks before going home. When I walked out to my car, 2 men approached me. I knew something was about to happen. One grabbed my keys and the other grabbed me by the arm and led me to a truck. He put a pillowcase over my head and told me to lay down on the seat. I heard him tell the other guy to take my car and follow him. I was so scared and crying. The man didn't talk to me. At some point, I knew we were on a dirt road and going up the mountain. When the truck stopped, I was led into a house and down some steps. He took off the pillow case. It was a nice basement area of a house. I asked why he was doing this but he never answered me. He handcuffed my wrists together to the bed frame and told me to go to sleep. All I could do was lay there wondering what was happening."

"What about the other man? Did you see him anymore?"

"No, I really don't even remember what he looked like. He never came to that house." Myra answered.

"After a couple of days, Natalie was brought there. I don't know who brought her because the one who stayed with me, went up the stairs and led her back down with a pillowcase over her head. When he took it off, I recognized her from the store. She was crying and looking around and asking what was happening. That man would give us water and sandwiches and then handcuff us back to the bed. I lost track of time and the days. I'm not sure how long we were there. One morning, he put the pillow cases over our heads and put us in the truck. We drove for maybe an hour and then we were put on a plane. He kept the pillow cases on our heads, we had no idea where we landed. When he took them off our heads, we were in a room with other women in a big house. I could hear others down the hall too. We knew we were in a tropical location because we could see palm trees out the window. We knew we were on at least the second floor and not the ground level." Myra paused and stared for a few seconds as if picturing the scene in her head.

"Did you ever hear the name of the man who took you and stayed with you and Natalie at the house and on the plane?" Reggie asked.

"No, he didn't talk and no one ever came down the steps except him so we didn't hear anyone talking to him or saying any names."

"Can you describe this man?" "Yes, I can." Myra answered.

Reggie held up a photo of Rum Mason. "Is this the man?"

"No, that's not him. I don't know who that is, I have never seen him. Who is he?" Myra asked.

"The man in the photo is Rum Mason. We know he is the person responsible for a large international trafficking ring. He actually has a house on the mountain in Birch Creek." Reggie explained.

"I haven't heard his name nor seen him at all."

"Myra, I believe you and Natalie were at Rum's house in his basement." Reggie was surprised that Myra had not seen nor heard his name.

"Is this the man who was with you?" Reggie held up a photo of Woody showing it to Myra. "No, I have never seen him either." she said.

"That's interesting, Woody must have been assigned to Kendra and this other guy was assigned to you and Natalie." Reggie was looking over at the FBI agent.

"Can we get someone to draw a description of this guy who seemed to be with Myra and Natalie?" He nodded in agreement.

"We will need to get Natalie's description of him too." He said.

"Isn't Kendra the girl that was missing before me? Did you find her?" Myra asked. "Yes, we did. She is back at home now and recovering from some injuries."

Myra had tears in her eyes.

"I'm so glad she was found too and will be ok. I don't think she was ever at the same place we were being held, at least I never saw Kendra. We had about 10 girls in our room and we could hear others in the other rooms down the hall. The girls in our room were all from different states, mostly Florida. They kept telling us that we were going to be shipped to another country on one of those big cargo ships and sold for trafficking. I kept telling myself, no, I wasn't going to be shipped to another country. I didn't even know what country I was in but I had a feeling I was going to be ok. Natalie wasn't as optimistic but I kept telling her we were going to be ok." Myra was crying as she described this situation.

Natalie sat quietly with her eyes closed while she waited to be interviewed. Reggie watched through the glass before entering the room. She felt sure Natalie would leave Birch Creek and return to Tennessee. Natalie had already given the description of the man who stayed with her and Myra until they landed in the Bahamas.

"Natalie, are you ready to talk?" Reggie asked as she sat down in the chair across from her. "Yes, I'm ready." She sighed.

"Tell us about the morning you were taken. Take as much time as you need to tell us and you can take a break whenever you need to." Reggie nodded her head towards the FBI agent to start recording.

"I was walking to work down the hill towards the store like I do every morning. I saw a truck turn by the store coming slowly up the hill. I watched it and then crossed the street to get closer to the store. When it stopped, I took a photo and started running towards the store. A man grabbed me and I threw my phone. I knew he was going to take it from me. When it landed on the roof, I think he gave up trying to get it. He put a pillowcase over my head and made me get into the truck. It happened so fast, I think I was in shock. He drove to a house and that is where I saw Myra. When he took the pillow case off, I saw her sitting on a bed. I knew we were kidnapped but it didn't make sense to me. I knew my family didn't have money to pay a ransom." Natalie explained.

"Tell me what the man looked like who grabbed you at the store."

"I really didn't get a good look at him, he had light blonde hair, medium height and weight. I don't remember anything specific, it happened so fast and then he put the pillow case on me. I never saw him again after I was taken to the house. He never said anything to me either. I kept asking what was going on but he never talked. Another man, the one I described to the artist, is who we saw for several days. He brought us sandwiches and water. He never spoke to us either. I don't know if he spoke English or not. Then, a few days later, he put the pillow cases back on us and we were taken to the plane and flew to that place where you found us."

Natalie started crying and thanking Reggie for rescuing them. "We can take a break, I will get you something to drink. "

Reggie needed a break too. She couldn't imagine the fear the girls had not knowing what was happening.

Reggie walked back in with the photos of Rum and Woody. "Natalie, do you recognize either of these two men?" "No, I haven't seen either one of them."

"Have you heard the name Rum or Woody mentioned?" Reggie asked. Natalie shook her head no.

"Alright, Natalie, I can't wait for you and Myra to go home and see your family. We will be leaving soon.

The FBI agent spoke up and thanked her for all the information and explained the drawing of the man they identified will be run through their database. If we identify who we think he is, we will ask you to identify as well.

"Okay", Natalie was nodding her head.

CHAPTER 36

Myra and Natalie's families met us at the airport. Watching the two girls embrace their parents and others was extremely emotional and also a moment Reggie would never forget. She stood observing those families. You could see the love they had for each other. Reggie was watching all of them when she looked over and saw TJ watching her. He smiled and embraced her.

"I love you, Regina Ann Memphis." "I love you too TJ Jenkins."

"Let's get you home," he said. "And where would that be?"

"Your home is wherever I am, I hope." he said, raising his eyebrows. Reggie knew at that moment she wanted to be with TJ forever. He was her family now.

"That sounds like the best home I could ever imagine." Reggie smiled and kissed his cheek. "I have a car and driver waiting for us."

As Reggie and TJ started to leave, she looked over at the girls and their families. She waved goodbye. Myra's father came over and hugged her.

"Detective Memphis, You are our hero, thank you so much for bringing our girl home safely.

You are the best." He said.

TJ shook his hand and said, "I couldn't agree more, she is the best."

The driver was standing out beside the limousine which was parked right out front. Once again, Reggie felt like a celebrity with such first class treatment. They circled around the airport to a gate with a guard house. The driver showed some papers and the gates opened.

"Are we getting on your plane now?" Reggie asked. "Yes, I have a surprise. "

Once they boarded the plane, he poured some champagne.

"Reggie, you have worked so hard on this case and now rescued those girls. You have endured so much in such a short amount of time but it is paying off. Rum isn't caught yet but eventually he will be. This case has caused you pain but it also brought us together. I know we haven't known each other that long but I have no doubts about our relationship. I hope you don't either."

"I have no doubts or regrets," she said.

"Reggie, I hope you don't mind but we are going to St. Simons Island for a few days." "Mind? That sounds like heaven to me." Reggie said.

She sat drinking her champagne. Her shoulders and neck no longer felt tense. How could it get any better than this? She thought.

They landed at a small airport on St, Simons Island. Another car and driver were waiting for them as they exited the plane. It was only a short drive to the most magnificent beach house she had ever seen.

"Wow it is breathtaking," she marveled, her eyes widened in awe as they turned into the circular drive. The grandeur of the estate overwhelmed her.

"This is where we'll be staying?" She inquired, a tinge of excitement in her voice.

TJ nodded with a knowing smile, leading her through the ornate front door. As she stepped inside, her gaze was drawn to the panoramic view beyond - the ocean stretching out before her, shimmering in the sunlight. She stood on the back deck soaking it all in.

TJ came out after a few minutes. She could feel the warm sun and smell the beachy air. She loved it and finally felt like she could breathe. The beach was beautiful and private. She didn't see anyone else out on the beach. She thought about taking her shoes off and running out there.

"Reggie, close your eyes and hold out your hand." he instructed gently. Trusting him, she complied. She heard a jingling noise and wondered what he was doing. He placed the object in her hand and told her to open her eyes.

"Keys? What are these for?" She inquired, her heart racing with anticipation.

"I bought this house, it is yours," he revealed, his voice filled with warmth and love.

Her lifelong dream of owning a beach house had finally come true, thanks to the generosity and thoughtfulness of the one she cherished most.

"Am I dreaming?" Reggie whispered in disbelief.

"How do I deserve this?" she murmured. As the reality of the moment sunk in, Reggie's heart swelled with love.

"This is mine? You mean ours," she said.

"This is home." He said as he dropped down to his knee. Time seemed to stand still.

Reggie's breath caught in her throat as he spoke her name with a tenderness that melted her heart.

"Regina Ann Memphis, Will you marry me?" He opened the box showing the most beautiful diamond ring she had ever seen.

"Yes, yes, yes!"

He stood, slid the ring on her finger and kissed her. She could feel her whole body tingling. "I have to be the happiest person on earth right now. How do I deserve you?" She was hugging him and admiring the gorgeous ring.

"I have one more surprise. Come inside with me."

"I'm not sure I can handle any more surprises today." She laughed.

He showed her to the bedroom. Reggie heard a familiar "meow."

Sammy was laying at the foot of the bed like he knew it was now his home and his bed.

"Oh my goodness, Sammy, I have missed you so much. TJ, Thank you, This day couldn't be any better! I love you,"

<h1 style="text-align:center">CHAPTER 37
SIX MONTHS LATER</h1>

Reggie and TJ were living in their house on St. Simon's Island, planning their wedding. TJ was writing his books that he had dreamed of for several years. Reggie was no longer employed with the Birch Creek Sheriff's office but volunteering at the local crisis center for women. She missed Sheriff Johnson, Ed and others in Birch Creek but loved her new life with TJ. She was going to work as a consultant part-time with the FBI on the continued sex trafficking ring investigation.

Freddie's half brothers had been prosecuted and were doing time in jail, not enough time according to Reggie but she couldn't control what the judge ordered.

Kendra was working at the flooring Company and had become a public speaker telling her story of the kidnapping and escape. Myra had finished high school early and was planning to attend Georgia Tech University. Natalie did move back to Tennessee to be with her brother and parents. Reggie didn't blame her for not wanting to stay in Birch Creek after what she had endured.

As much time and attention the FBI had put into trying to arrest and prosecute Rum, they had not been able to yet. No one would agree to testify against him and they didn't have enough evidence to tie him to what had happened. Some of his employees had been prosecuted but he was too smart to get caught. None of the kidnapped and recovered girls had ever seen Rum nor knew of him even though the FBI knew he was the leader. They weren't giving up but said it could take years to actually arrest him. Rum was keeping a low profile these days for fear of being killed by his ex-employees and fear of being arrested. Reggie knew he would turn up or make a big mistake at some point and she would be helping the FBI to arrest him. He was the missing link.

TJ and Reggie were working on a book together to tell the story of the mystery of Birch Creek. TJ had sold the Jenkins Corporation and received his asking price. Reggie had never dreamed of living this type of lifestyle and felt so blessed to have met TJ and knew it was meant to be.

The doorbell rang, Reggie yelled to TJ that she would answer it.

Reggie opened the front door seeing a man with a large bag hanging from his shoulder. "Hello, I'm Nick. Nick Daniels. I'm your wedding planner." He smiled.

"Come in, nice to meet you. My fiance's sister spoke so highly of your work. She attended a fundraiser event you planned in New York a few months back."

As Reggie was walking him inside to sit down, she kept staring at his familiar face.

"You look so familiar to me but I can't place where I might have seen you. I can't wait to see the ideas you have in store for our wedding." Reggie said. Nick smiled.

"I have been highlighted in some wedding magazines and articles so that may be how you recognize me."

Nick quickly answered wanting to change the subject. Rum had convinced Nick that Reggie would never know he was connected to him.

"I have great plans for your wedding, You will be blown away with my ideas." Nick smiled.

AUTHOR'S NOTE

When I first sat down to write *The Missing Link*, I had no idea where it would take me. Reggie Memphis was the first character who had taken root in my mind. She pushed me to tell her story. She came to me as a woman determined to prove herself, navigating a world that doesn't always take women seriously, especially in law enforcement.

This book is special to me because it was the beginning of my journey as a fiction author. *The Missing Link* was my first attempt at writing a full length mystery. I learned how to trust my voice and let my characters surprise me. I poured my heart into every twist and revelation, hoping it would do justice to the strength, fear and hope we all carry when searching for the truth.

If you're reading this as part of a book club, thank you. I wrote *The Missing Link* with discussion in mind. Beneath the crime and clues, this is a story about trust, trauma, and the bonds that either save us or break us. Thank you for being a part of this story. I hope Reggie and her journey stay with you long after the last page.

With gratitude,

JK Brogdon

MEET THE AUTHOR
JK BROGDON
Q&A

Q: What inspired you to write The Missing Link?

First a little of my background is in order - I am a social worker, human behavior fascinates me, I love true crime shows/movies, investigating and interviewing are my passions. So, why did I write *The Missing Link* - I have always been drawn to stories that combine suspense with emotion, where the mystery is as much about the characters as it is about the crime. Reggie came to me as a smart, determined woman with something to prove. I live in a small town which has many great landmarks and events that needed to be described in a book.

Q: How did you develop the character of Reggie Memphis?

Reggie is a mix of several people I know including some of myself. My sisters think Reggie is them. Reggie represents strength and vulnerability. She is a woman navigating a tough job while dealing with her own trauma. She's not perfect, but she is real. Once I started writing, her story just flowed out of me. I hope readers see part of themselves in her.

Q: What Challenges did you face while writing this book?

Everything! Many personal and professional challenges! As my debut fiction novel, I had to learn how to structure a mystery, build suspense, and trust that the story would unfold. The biggest challenge was not listening to self-doubt or negative self talk. I had to let go of perfection and allow the characters to lead the way. I rewrote sections more than once. Every revision brought me closer to how I wanted the story to play out. It took me about 1 ½ years to write this book. I would write and the words just flow. Other times, I would be stuck on where to go next and then the self-doubt would creep in. I took a lot of time to think about the characters and think about how to tell the story when I wasn't writing. I would put it away and sometimes it was weeks before I started to write again. That is probably not the best advice for any aspiring writers because everything I have learned from other writers says to just keep writing and write everyday.

Q: What do you hope readers take away from The Missing Link ?

I hope readers walk away feeling like they've been on an emotional ride. I hope they like the twists in the story and love the characters. This story is about truth, justice, courage and relationships. These characters protect, hide and fight. I hope it sparks thoughtful discussion in book clubs around some of the social issues in the world today-suicide, substance abuse, human trafficking, etc. I also hope it leaves the reader wanting more! *The Weakest Link* is the sequel.

Q: What's next for you?

The story continues in *The Weakest Link*, the sequel. It picks up with Reggie and TJ facing new threats. It's even more intense and layered than the first. Beyond Reggie and TJ, I'm working on new stories that blend suspense, emotion, and always strong women in complex situations. Each of my fiction books will be about a strong female character who has challenges and each book will have some social issues thrown into the mix. I'm just getting started!

THE MISSING LINK BOOK CLUB EDITION
DISCUSSION QUESTIONS

1. Reggie Memphis is driven by the need to prove herself. How does that shape her approach to the case? And to the people around her? Did her ambition help or hinder her?

2. What are the power dynamics between Reggie and Sheriff Johnson? How do you think their relationship reflects real challenges women face in law enforcement or male dominated fields?

3. How did your opinion of TJ change over the course of the book? Did you find him trustworthy? Why or Why Not?

4. The title, The Missing Link, has multiple meanings. What do you think it refers to?

5. Which plot twist or reveal surprised you the most? Were there any clues you caught early that turned out to be important?

6. Were there any characters you related to personally or felt strongly about. Positively or negatively? Why?

7. Do you think justice was served by the end? Why or why not?

8. What questions are you still left with at the end of the book?

9. What do you think will happen in the sequel - The Weakest Link?

Book Club Edition Exclusive:

Here is your sneak peak at the first 2 chapters of The Weakest Link.

THE WEAKEST LINK

CHAPTER 1

"Eligible Bachelor, Terrence J. Jenkins is now taken by a small town girl, Regina Ann Memphis, to be wed in Birch Creek" - This was the headline in the social column of the Chicago News Tribune. TJ and Reggie's photo was posted under the headline. It was taken at the green space dedication ceremony, when Reggie took her first trip to Chicago. As Reggie stared at the photo, she couldn't believe how much time had already passed since that day.

"TJ, come here and look!" Reggie was smiling at TJ as he entered the room.

"What is it?"

"Looks like I just won the prize, I got the most eligible bachelor in Chicago!" She reached over to kiss him.

"When did I become the most eligible bachelor?" he laughed.

"I bet all the Chicago socialites are wondering where the hell is Birch Creek?"

"They didn't print the date of the wedding did they?" TJ was concerned about the possibility of Rum Mason hearing about their wedding.

"No, it doesn't say. It mostly talks about you and your family and how much they are estimating you to be worth."

TJ rolled his eyes. Reggie smiled knowing how lucky she is to be marrying him. The thought had not crossed her mind about Rum finding out about their plans. As she stared at the article, her mind went back to the day she helped rescue Myra and Natalie. She will never forget the look in their eyes, the conditions all those girls were living in, how scared they all must have been. Three girls from her hometown, Birch Creek, were taken to be sold and trafficked by evil men who worked for Rumsfeld Mason, the most evil of them all! He had the largest human trafficking ring in the world but now it had been mostly destroyed. Reggie smiled as she remembered how all of the community in Birch Creek came together to help find Kendra, Myra and Natalie. TJ had brought in all the major news sources which helped the nation to be informed of what was going on in their small town. And then, the wonderful observant nurse in Savannah who realized Kendra was the unidentified patient he had laying in a coma in the ICU. Most of Rum's men had been arrested in connection with this world-wide trafficking network.

Several were arrested the day Reggie and the FBI found all the girls, including Myra and Natalie, at the compound in the Bahamas. Rum had not been found nor had the FBI been able to find any of his employees willing to give him up, actually, most didn't even know him. Rum had a calculating way of not being linked to any of it even though he was the one calling all the shots. He made everyone else do his dirty work.

"Reggie, did you hear what I said?" TJ asked.

"No, sorry, I was daydreaming about all that happened since the day that photo of us was taken. I want Rum caught and we have to figure out how to find him."

TJ sat next to her looking her in the eyes.

"Once he is caught, the FBI has to figure out how to link him to all of this. I know you have made it your mission to find him but don't let it take over your life. We have a wedding to plan and a wonderful life to live. Reggie, you did your job by finding the three missing girls from your hometown, mystery solved, remember?" He was serious about her being able to move on.

"I hear you and I love you. You ground me and protect me." She hugged him knowing that he meant well.

Right on cue, Sammy meowed and jumped up into her lap.

"And Sammy brings me back to reality. I'm going to take that as a sign. How did I get so lucky to be marrying you, have the best cat ever and be living on St. Simon's island in a magnificent house on the beach?"

"Reggie, you deserve everything in the world. Let me give it to you." TJ grabbed her hand kissing it.

CHAPTER 2

Rum Mason was still laying low somewhere in Europe. The exact location remained a mystery to everyone-everyone, that is, except his lover, Nick. For the last couple of weeks, Nick had been handling all the wedding plans for Reggie and TJ.

"Rum, I miss you so much! I hope I can see you soon."

"I miss you too."

It was too dangerous for them right now; any hint of their connection could expose them both. Rum had been a ghost for months, slipping through the hands of the FBI. Once a powerful figure who operated in the shadows, he was now the prime suspect in the largest human trafficking ring ever uncovered. He was the missing link and the FBI and Reggie still had no concrete evidence to tie him to this ring other than knowing exactly that he was the leader.

Federal agents had dismantled most of the network but Rum remained hidden. He had orchestrated everything from afar, leaving no direct evidence of his involvement. Even in hiding, Rum's need for control and revenge burned brighter than ever.

"Nick, call me after your meeting, we need to finalize their wedding reception finale." Rum laughed. His laugh was evil. He wanted to destroy any chance of Reggie finding him.

"Oh ok," Nick hesitated. He would do almost anything Rum asked of him but he didn't want to be in charge of hurting anyone.

"I've got to go. Talk later."

As Nick was ending the call, Reggie appeared in the doorway of the Birch Creek Chapel, the soft glow of the late afternoon light streaming through the stained glass windows. She was back in the town where it all began, at the place where she had always dreamed of saying her vows. Marrying TJ here would be her dream come true. As a young girl, when her parents were fighting and drinking causing chaos, she would run to this very chapel. She would sit on the creaky wooden pews. She would stare up at the kaleidoscope of colors cast by the windows and dream of her prince who would whisk her away to his castle. Now, standing here as a grown woman she was going to marry her prince soon. She took a deep breath letting the cool country air feel her lungs. She realized even though she had her prince, he hadn't rescued her; he had simply reminded her she had the courage to rescue herself.

"Hello Nick, I hope you didn't have any trouble finding this chapel way out here in the country." Reggie was walking towards the front of the church looking up at the beautiful wooden beams and the large stained glass windows. It all looked just as she remembered it.

"No, my GPS actually led me right to it. I assume this chapel has some sort of sentimental value to you? It looks like it hasn't been occupied in years."

Reggie ignored his question. She didn't want to share her reasons as to why she chose this chapel.

"TJ and I want the wedding to be intimate and very special with our family and friends sharing our day with us." Reggie sat down in the front pew as Nick was pulling out his plans.

"A Fall wedding is always so beautiful with cooler temperatures and the sun setting by six o'clock. When the wedding begins, the church will have a soft glow, lit up by candlelight.

Candles everywhere! No lights. The shimmering candles will be magnificent!" Nick showed Reggie a photo of the candles he was wanting to use.

"That looks beautiful. I want to caution you that we don't want to cause any sort of fire hazard."

"You let me handle all of that. Of course, I will make sure you approve everything." He smiled nervously knowing it wasn't going to be her dream wedding after all. Nick showed her all his ideas for the decor inside and outside of the chapel. Nick was careful not to show her the plans for the reception just yet. Reggie didn't know about the huge pavilion TJ was having built down by the river for the wedding reception. TJ had purchased the property as a wedding gift for Reggie. Nick wasn't going to bring up the reception for fear he would accidentally spoil the surprise.

"We decided on the caterer. It will be from TJ's favorite restaurant in Chicago. We still don't know yet where to have the reception, I'm going to check out a few places while I'm here in town."

"Oh ok, let me know as soon as you pick the place."

We aren't having a wedding cake because we want my friend Darlene to make all of her special pies. Nobody ever eats wedding cake anyway!"

Nick was thinking how tacky that sounded but wasn't going to tell Reggie. He would make it all elegant looking even if it was some hometown pies. He was getting to know Reggie and liked her so far. Her accent was special. He loved hearing her say, "Bless your heart."

"Where has the time gone?" Reggie was looking at her watch.

"Nick, I have to go meet someone. We can talk later about where to have the reception?" Nick was pulling out his tape measure.

"Yes, I'm just going to stay here for a few more minutes and take some measurements."

He wanted to walk down the path to the river to see the progress being made on the pavilion. He knew it was going to be beautiful.

"Ok, talk to you soon." Reggie left.

As soon as Reggie was out of sight, Nick walked down by the river to see the pavilion. There was no pavilion yet. The lot had been graded and concrete poured but that was all. The square footage had been marked off and flagged. River Birch trees lined the river making a shaded canopy over the water. Maybe he could put some lights in the trees to make it look more festive, he thought to himself. He really wanted it to look like an enchanted forest and be a dream wedding for Reggie. Rum does not need to be interfering with their wedding. What good will that do? It will only get him caught. He will convince Rum to leave it alone.